I

SLAUGHTERMATIC

By Steve Aylett

Four Walls Eight Windows
New York

© 1998 Steve Aylett

Published in the United States by:

Four Walls Eight Windows
39 West 14th Street, room 503
New York, N.Y., 10011

Visit our website at http://www.fourwallseightwindows.com

First printing March 1997.

Library of Congress Cataloging-in-Publication Data:

Aylett, Steve.
Slaughtermatic/ by Steve Aylett
p. cm.
ISBN 1-56858-103-3
I. Title.
PR6051.Y57S58 1998
823'.914—dc21   97-41132
                              CIP

Text design by Ink, Inc.

10 9 8 7 6 5 4 3 2 1

Printed in Canada

to Victoria

"I think I'm hit."
—*Baby Face Nelson,*
hit seventeen times by a .45 caliber Tommy gun.

CONTENTS

BEERLIGHT
xi

I
THE HOLDUP
1

2
THE LOOSE END
53

3
THE INFERNO
107

Beerlight was a blown circuit, where to kill a man was less a murder than a mannerism. Every major landmark was a pincushion of snipers. Cop tanks navigated a graffiti-rashed riot of needle bars, oil-scabbed neon and diced rubble. Fragile laws were shattered without effort or intent and the cops considered false arrest a moral duty. Integrity was no more than a fierce dream. Crime was the new and only art form. The authorities portrayed shock and outrage but never described what it was they had been expecting. Anyone trying to adapt was persecuted. One woman had given birth to a bulletproof child. Other denizens were bomb zombies, pocketing grenades and wandering gaunt and vacant for days before winding down and pulling the pin on themselves. There was no beach under the sidewalk.

Yet in dealing with this environment the one strategy common to all was the assumption that it could be dealt with.

PART I

THE HOLDUP

Dante Cubit pushed into the bank, thinking about A. A. Milne. Why didn't he ever write *Now We Are Dead*? No foresight, Dante decided. Always think ahead. Under Dante's full-length coat was an old 10-gauge Winchester, an Uzi machine pistol and a Zero Approach handgun. Against his heart was a thesaurus bound in PVC. He smiled at the entrance guard.

The bank was huge. He'd never been here but knew every inch of the place from rehearsals in a computer simulation—the weirdest part was that it lacked the virtual glow which made everything come on like a precious gem.

At the rear wall he saw the Entropy Kid gnashing painkillers and messing with a euthanasia form. The Kid was almost amphibious with despair, in his orderly way. He'd once studied deterioration in order to have something definite to tell folks when they asked why he was sobbing. Then science discovered that the universe's shape was a downward spiral and he took it to heart. Five minutes before Dante, he had swanned into the bank like an angel on stabilizers. Inside his jacket was a Kafkacell cannon gun. He gave Dante a covert nod and eyed a slab-head guard who was trying to appear as devoid of emotion as he'd soon become.

Dante approached the customer interface. He'd thought of modulating his voice but since meeting Rosa Control he'd engaged in so much oral sex his accent had changed.

He pulled the machine pistol, talking low. "Hands up,

granddad, and no sudden moves—it's a money or your life paradigm."

"Eh?" said the kind-faced gent behind the glass.

"It's a stickup, old man."

"Excuse me?"

"Okay gimme a minute here." Dante consulted the thesaurus. "Okay, we got heist, holdup, robbery, raid and, er, 'demanding money with menaces.'"

"Right, got ya. Did you say no sudden moves?"

"Correct."

"So you wouldn't want me to do—*this*?"

"Hey I ain't kiddin—"

"Or puff my cheeks out abruptly—like *this*?"

"Hey now don't be doin' that—"

"I guess we're on the same wavelength, sir," the oldster relented cheerfully. "But hey now when you use the quaint expression, 'Your money or your life,' I reckon you mean my money or my life *and* my money."

"What?"

"Lemme get this straight, young man—you're proposing to ventilate me and take the money if I don't hand it over?"

"That's right, yeah."

"So you'll either take the money, or both my life *and* the money?"

"Sure, I guess that's right. Your money, or your life *and* your money."

"But it ain't my money."

"What'd you say?"

"Ain't the bank's neither—belongs to the customer till the bank invests in a bum deal and crashes, foreclosing on the setup and leaving the customer without a pot to piss in."

"Ain't that illegal?"

"Sure—till it happens."

"Okay, let's see if I understand this—the bank uses the customer's money for investment."

"No it doesn't—uses its own money. When d'you ever find your credit balance reduced because the bank manager lent it out or invested it someplace?"

"Never. How about that."

"Hey Danny," whispered the Entropy Kid, edging over.

"Wait a mo', Kid. So listen, how does the cash newt?"

"Think about it," said the teller in a tone of gentle encouragement. "The only investment cash the bank takes from the customer is payment interest and charges."

"My deposit's sittin' pretty?"

"Right," nodded the teller, delighted with Dante's progress.

"Danny," hissed the Kid, pulling at Dante's sleeve. "We got work."

"Listen to this guy, Kid—so what you're saying," Dante asked the teller, "is despite the bank using its own money to back up lending and investment, it's the customer's cash it draws on when the shit hits the fan."

"Exactly—supported by the myth that banks do business by relending and investing the customer's funds. They even draw up their books with depositors' and borrowers' sums on either side of the balance sheet."

"No shit. You hear this, Kid? No shit."

"Yeah, that's great Danny," the Kid coughed.

"I don't believe it," Dante was saying, dazed. "My great granddaddy *died* in the Depression."

"That's a *shame*," said the teller with real compassion.

A perky, gum-chewing teller strode brightly up to the old guy. "Slips to sign, Mr. Kraken," she said, then saw Dante's gun and shrieked, dropping everything.

"For god's sake Corey," complained the old guy. The rear guard pulled a gun and the Kid's Kafkacell went off like a grenade, putting the guard through the wall—a shell the size of a silencer flew against the teller window. The front guard spun with a snub repeater and the Kid blew him into the street in an explosion of glass.

The Kid backed across the marble floor, brandishing the cannon gun twitchily. "Keep a cool cortex nobody gets hurt," he whispered.

"What'd he say?" squinted Mr. Kraken.

"He says keep a cool cortex, nobody'll get hurt—means everyone, everyone's cortexes. And that includes the inner matter of the cerebrum itself. The Kid's got a speech problem, but he's okay. Ain't that right, Kid?"

"Tell 'em to keep off the tills, Danny," whispered the Kid.

"Yeah keep off the pills, ladies and gentlemen—it's a slippery slope and you know it. Kraken, you the head teller, right? Get in back and chip the vault."

This was fine by Mr. Kraken—even lazy flies with no vested interest in anything had participated in the festival of alarm-tripping which Dante's gun had triggered. The old man chuckled to himself and shuffled along so slowly that paleontologists were pouring plaster into his tracks. Dante and the Kid put their heads together. "Must have been a glacier in a past life, Danny."

"Yeah, lucky we ain't really after cash—this rate, it won't be worth shit after inflation."

"Denizens at the door, Danny."

Passersby were standing on the oblonged guard and peering in through the shattered entrance. Cop sirens were howling. "Quit stallin' old man," shouted Dante. "Gimme the key."

Dante left the Kid on guard and took the keychip into the vault room.

The vault was on a time lock—when the chip was used

without the correct combination the user was thrown twenty minutes into a future in which he or she was already cuffed and surrounded. The computer man, Download Jones, had hacked a card swiper which was now housed in Dante's belt buckle—Dante swiped it through, altering the program. He pushed it into the lock, tapped out a random set of numbers and was thrown twenty minutes into the past.

The sirens cut out instantly. Nobody knew he was in the vault room. He had ten minutes before the Entropy Kid entered the bank, and fifteen before he himself did.

Rosa Control had excised the real combination from the manager by threatening to cut off his hand, and because his palmprint was also required, had cut off his hand. Dante thumped the hand against the print panel and tapped in the code—the door clanked. He pushed at it like a stalled car and it slowly swung.

Dante went immediately to a deposit hatch, opening it with a tension wrench and rake pick. Inside was a book bound in PVC. He removed it and placed his ballast thesaurus and the hand in its place, closing the hatch. Leaving the vault and swinging closed the heavy metal door, he sat at the depositors' table and fired up the volume with a mixture of tense excitement and reverence:

Life and death have equal authority in nature. When laws contradict so fundamentally they cause mere confusion in the average soul—rarely a clean break. Yet when two principles meet which can't be reconciled the intervening space is perfect for demonstrations of balloon-folding and fart ignition. In the right place and at the right time it's possible to gall both the non-evolving head of the fascist and the dilute mind of the vapid liberal. Opposites attract, resulting in a narrowing of possibilities. Explosions amplify

in an enclosed space. People say that those who attack a
system should be prepared to live without it and assume
they are not. The worst thing about the ogre in a
nightmare is having to dispose of its corpse.

Satisfied, he stood and tucked the book into his pants. He found a fuse box and blinded the bank floor cameras with a boltcutter. Waiting just inside the vault room he watched the clock and idly thought of how a jester's costume of matching halves was a handy guide for sawing. Then he entered the bank floor and pressed the Uzi to the rear guard's temple. "Drop the guzzler."

The Entropy Kid was nearby gnashing painkillers and messing with a euthanasia form. The guard's gun clattered to the floor and the Kid looked up, jittery and startled. Dante saw the Kid's fear in all its polychrome ferment—from the jug of his skull poured a spine of unset Jell-O. "This the second time for you, Danny? How'd I do?"

A commotion at the entrance—the front guard had drawn and been grabbed from behind—shots cracked off into the ceiling, blowing lights. Tellers screamed. The guard was knocked cold by the newcomer, who stepped forward and spread his arms casually wide. He wore a full-length coat, three shades of black. Dante again. "Hell's other people, Cubit," he said, "especially when they're gassing you."

Dante raised the Winchester, and hesitated.

Dante Two took another step forward. Alarms were clamoring. "Spill, Cubit. We agreed."

Dante aimed and Dante Two threw an arm across his eyes. The rifle clicked, jammed—Dante Two peeked.

Dante squeezed again and shot him in the belly. Dante Two doubled over and keeled onto the floor.

"You—Corey, that your name? You're a hostage."

Dante dragged Corey the Teller toward the rear exit as the Entropy Kid kept the Kafka on the assembly. The three backed out.

"You must be mortified," Corey shrieked, chewing gum. "You shot your own twin *brudder*?"

"Wasn't Danny's brudder, miss," whispered the Kid as they rushed through the vault room, "it was Danny."

"Most guys leave prints on the scene," chewed Corey as Dante wired the elevator. "You leave a whole body back there?"

"We never leave no prints," said the Kid. "Always quality hand-brushed originals with us, eh Danny?"

"I'm legally dead, miss," Dante explained. The elevator opened and they stepped in. "My Ma gets the insurance. No music, thank Christ—got any gum?"

Corey handed Dante a stick and they chewed in unison as the elevator ascended. The Kid grabbed a handful of pills from his pocket and banged them into his mouth.

"Stay alert," said Dante.

"Painkillers are the drugs of the future, Danny."

"Sure, but you ain't gonna see it," Corey muttered, and blew a huge pink bubble.

On the third floor Dante used the gum to stick a charge to the console and sent the elevator down. The three started along a hallway and, as the floor thumped with the explosion, Dante stopped short at a wall which shouldn't have been there.

He and the Kid knew every turn of the place due to walk-throughs in VR—Download Jones had done a beautiful job from a set of architect's plans off the dredge. But it was dawning on Dante that aside from the bank itself the simulation was a drooper. It seemed Jones had used the wrong schematic. They'd memorized the wrong building.

A contagion of squad cars moved between the potholes of Deal Street like roaches prowling a cheap hotel. In Beerlight this was a risk—so many were boosted the authorities had considered replacing them with a monorail. The reflection of code art and graffiti scrolled across a window behind which a figure was bent in thought or indigestion. A random bullet spiderwebbed the window, erasing the image.

It was the last car to pull up in the twilight shadow of the Deal Street Highrise. The door opened and Chief Henry Blince bulged out like a gum bubble which refused to burst. Blince had lost all sense of proportion—each of his chins was registered to vote. His bulk was the only thing standing between justice and chaos, and he had so far kept these conditions innocent of one another. Biting into a doughnut the size of a flotation ring, he surveyed the first floor bank. "How many inside, Benny?"

"Twenty-five, Chief," sniggered Benny the Trooper.

"How many outside?"

"Four and a half million, Chief, border to border."

"And ain't it right that every one of us is essentially bisexual?"

"That's what they say, Chief."

"So us and the folks inside'll have somethin' to talk about. Gimme the bullhorn." The bullhorn screeched like a stuck pig as Blince aimed it at the bank. "Come out and we won't blow the whistle on your goddamn depravities. Dogs? Cattle? Who'll ever know? And for those o' you with Oedipal urges, mom's the word."

Blince broke off to gasp with laughter. Benny was kicking the car with constricted mirth.

"Now why ain't they emergin', Benny?"

"It's the sirens, Chief—they know who we are."

"That so?" Blince raised the bullhorn. "Fractal eddies, you sons o' bitches. Everythin' influences everythin' else. You're goddamn accessories and I got hard scientific evidence."

"Non-linearity's six feet under, Chief."

"You pitchin' complexity? Hell with that—all I need's a bagel and a caffeine drip."

"Nah, disorder theory, Chief—'Every action or inaction may or may not be related to some other action or inaction.'"

"By any other dumb name, Benny, and just where in the wide world d'*you* leap off tellin' *me* what's the fashion? With your pewter pants. This here's a clean-up operation, Benny. We're at the crime face, drillin' on all cylinders. Stampin' on the many and varied serpent heads o' subversion. Born to the job while the smoke o' creation was still swirlin'."

Benny giggled and pranced on the spot. "I got a good feelin' about this, Chief."

"You and me both, Benny."

"I'm beefed up."

"Me too, Benny, me too. Get a demographic cannon out here and put it on a broad setting."

At that moment a figure emerged through the shattered entrance, shuffling and decrepit, hands timidly raised. "What's the point o' this joker?" asked Blince. The town and its people were found wanting in the harsh glare of his ignorance. "Gimme your guzzler, Benny."

Benny handed over a snub gun and Blince whirled the chamber, spitting aside like a pitcher on a mound. Then he shuttered and raised the gun. Mr. Kraken was cut in half like a credit card.

The Kid went over to the third floor window. "This place, man," he breathed. "Reminds me what my pa said on his deathbed."

"What'd he say?" asked Corey.

"Nuthin', miss—he was dead. Hey Danny, there's cops out here and the sun's goin' down."

"Terrific," said Dante, peering at the ceiling. "Here I've taken responsibility for four lives and the brotherhood wants to relieve me of the consequences." Dante emptied the Winchester into the ceiling, threw it aside and pulled a desk across the floor. "I see Download again I'm gonna tease a bullet into his head. Easier to pull a hat out of a rabbit than a habit out of a rat."

Download Jones had a reputation as a practical joker. He liked to put scorpions on people's seats and look on as these rarest of animals were crushed. Like most socketeers his worldview was small format. He'd siphoned his brain into a mainframe which would have stupid ideas even after his death. He was a youth excited too often by the future.

"Download wouldn't dump us," whispered the Kid as the three climbed through the ceiling. "Deep down he's all heart—stab him and the knife'd germinate."

Dante had the job down to fly-leg detail. The first three floors belonged to the bank and the bank's elevator rose no further. Above that, according to Download's sensurround reconstruction, were seventeen floors devoted to scams of every stamp, reached by a bullet elevator up the side of the building. Dante's little group would hitch the bullet to the roof where Rosa Control would be waiting with a grin and a jetfoil to Alaska—the continuation of Dante's life and reputation would be assured. He and the Kid were pioneers of the permutation heist, forcing staff to sample small cakes or listen to dismal poetry. They stole trashbaskets, flooded vaults with kelp sludge and staged full costume drama for nocturnal surveillance cameras. Tonight's piece was meant to launch the more subtle and mature work for which everyone assured them they were ready.

On the fourth floor they found a warehouse full of hydraulic dictators and other creepy toys. The bullet elevator didn't show but there was a regular one the brotherhood had taken out with a crowdpleaser. "Why'd they run a tank into the elevator?" gasped Corey.

"Didn't figure we newted the other one," said Dante. "Guess they know we're headed for the roof."

"I hate inflatables!" Corey shrieked, kicking the face of a vinyl Hitler. "They're historic!"

Dante was already feeling strange about the caper— about everything. Was it just the screwup with the building? By guesswork he tried to match his disassociation to the disused words he'd salvaged from a contraband copy of *Vampire Reverse*. Abandonment? Jacinth? Shame? Nostalgia?

He seated himself against a wall and breathed deeply. For once he was glad Rosa wasn't around—she referred to meditation as "aspirin on stilts" and approved less of the rom book he'd boosted from the vault: *The Impossible Plot of Biff Barbanel* by Eddie Gamete.

He visualized the waters of a pond until the last of the shark fins had submerged. A little clearer in the head, he closed the meditation and scrolled the stolen volume, recalling the story. Biff Barbanel is a diametric prankster who, chagrined at the microscopic impact created by even the grandest actions of the individual, sets upon a campaign of experimentation to determine the largest results attainable by the smallest personal effort. He wires up a sophisticated sonic rig to record himself blinking and relay the sound through ten stack amplifiers in the front yard, so that the slightest flicker of an eyelid shatters windows up and down the street. He changes a lightbulb by holding it up and letting the world revolve around him. He writes a history of digitotalitarianism by assigning letters of the alphabet to the varied unreachable itches in his middle ear. He officially nominates a "slight, fleeting sensation of nausea" as a senatorial candidate. He declares a ceasefire with his reflection. Having learned to effect the world in a grain of sand and create heaven in a wildflower, he goes into the larger world with a tortuously amplified causal energy and finds he can switch the world image to negative and positive and back again with the flick of a hand. Told in the first person, the entire scenario proves to be the demented fantasy of a gameshow host who has repented and sits all day at the window wearing a propeller hat. "A thought is no different than an act," he concludes, "especially if your thoughts are of no consequence."

This was the last thing Gamete had written before his spectacular death. Legend had it the book had been written not with a pen but a bellows.

Dante knew all this from snaffle and hearsay, but now was the first time he'd held the fruit in his paws. Browsing, he saw straight off the story wasn't central—the spice seemed to be in the speed-of-consciousness rants Barbanel scrawls on the walls and ceiling:

> *There was a time when the extension of illegality to innocent acts could be used to manipulate men. But when guilt is no longer felt over acts of genuine criminality, what hope of instilling guilt in the innocent?*

Barbanel's wallworks reminded Dante of an exercise he'd idly pursued during rehearsal—as an installation piece the job had been organized more like a notion than an act. They'd memorized the upper floors in case the elevator stalled, but Dante was faster than the Kid and spent a lot of spare time creating a memory palace. Every hall and corner of the building was used as a signifier, a means of remembering text and images by having them dotted around the walls of the simulation. Strolling through the simulation he could read an entire story, and then, by walking through the real thing, be able to recall it.

But this wasn't the building he'd memorized—similarities and flashes of text were triggered here and there but in a jumbled order. He'd memorized a favorite Gamete story in which an angel stows away in a hypodermic needle and is inadvertently injected. The girl who receives it feels only the faintest tingle as the being is absorbed.

In this unfamiliar place the story was scrambled so that the girl was injected into the angel, which reacted by becoming a god. Why was the real thing different from the simulation? Had Jones really sold them down the river?

As he sat considering these issues he heard the leper's bell of an approaching idea—maybe Download never let them out of the simulation. The thought hit him like a car at a stop sign. If they were still hooked in, the heist had been nothing but a wraparound dream.

Virtual reality. That would explain why he felt so bored.

3 . ROSA

Rosa strode down Swerve Street, dragging her nails along the wall. Sparks leapt and underscored a graffiti saying *Only the expert will realize your exaggerations are true*. In her other hand was a Zero Approach gun identical to Dante's except for a squeeze adjustment—Rosa had lost a finger in a mood ring explosion. She couldn't believe she was here when Dante was waiting for the pickup on Deal Street. Download was up to no good. A guy like that needed a wound bigger than his body.

Developed to re-empower the victim, the Zero Approach gun worked on a principle of etheric consent and only fired when the target was asking for it. Since its introduction the homicide rate had risen by four hundred percent. Download's ignorance was sure to demand a bullet. Without the firm and necessary grasp of present and past, he didn't believe an entire nation could lie. She thundered over the monroe grill which served as a welcome mat for his digital foundry.

Dante thought of dolls within dolls and wheels within wheels. "Hey Kid—Kid. I look okay?"

"Yuh look like shit, Danny."

"Sure, but I ain't all shiny, right, not movin' like a robot?" He flexed his hand, viewing it. It seemed completely normal. "This look texture-mapped to you?"

The Kid ignored him, slumped morosely against a gas tank. He was thinking of a time when things were different as the result of an experiment. Hearing frequent news reports of people's unsuspecting and carefree condition just prior to violent misfortune, the Kid had attempted to attain this condition by taking out a contract on himself and ingesting an amnesia drug to forget the arrangement. Sure enough, on the day of the hit he felt an alien lightheartedness. But as the hitman's car sped toward him he remembered everything and felt more cheated than ever that others got the service for free. He leapt aside and the hitman, who hadn't a care in the world, died violently on impact with a wall.

Seating herself opposite him, Corey the Teller asked gently after his well-being. He raised a face scorched with reality and whispered that life would be great if it weren't for its termination in a box of earthworms. They got to talking about carrion, absence as therapy and the fact that not a single vitamin had ever been visually identified. The Kid described his ability to mentally unwind people like spiral-peeled apples and see them as skanking, swing-armed skeletons. "One thing you'll say for skeletons," Corey said brightly. "They'll always give you a smile." There are two ways of bringing someone around to your way of thinking—softly, or hardly.

"Danny says crime's one of many methods justice may select," the Kid quoted. "But I don't think I believe in justice—d'you, miss?"

"Far as I can in somethin' I never saw—so break it to me, you guys givin' up or what?"

"You think we're in Jones's fuzz machine, Danny?" asked the Kid, uneasy at Dante's suspicion that they weren't real crooks. "Still in them old-fashioned roller wheels?"

Dante gazed up from his book. "Chances are this heist ain't been accomplished Kid, just portrayed, like electoral hype."

The Kid was puzzled by his accomplice's apparent apathy—this wasn't the Dante he knew. The Dante he knew would spring into action so fast he'd leave his aura behind. Was this hanging around part of the plan? "What about intent, Danny?"

"Sure I guess we got that," Dante conceded, though he was on shaky ground. There was a name for those with intent to crime who subsequently enacted it in a simulation—crap.

In fact VR was held in such contempt that many states

ran hive jails in which prisoners were permanently hooked into a sim crime environment to play out their rage until decrepitude or drooling madness. Physically the prison was a coffin-stacked bunker, where inmates were drip-fed nutrients and urban fantasy.

It was a source of mirth throughout the SSA that the virtual environment, called the Mall, was modeled on Beerlight. This had led Beerlight itself to reject plans for a VR clench, opting instead for a re-offenders' trashpile and a standard clench for first-timers. The petty clench was based on the old panoptic model despite complaints from tower guards that every single prisoner would stare at them.

"Maybe we been arrested already, Danny. Wired up in one of them funny places."

"We'll find out at midnight," said Dante absently. He knew the Mall ran the same twenty-four hours on a loop and that there was a burst of static at the reset. Anyone killed was resurrected. Anything damaged was restored. Like a kid's game.

"What about *her*?" whispered the Kid, pointing at Corey.

Dante said nothing. If this was Jones's simulation she was no less a puppet than the toys in the warehouse—effectively, she was Jones.

None of it really accounted for the weirdness—since he worked the vault he'd been weaker, spread thin, in two minds about the whole match. He thought of *Rumpelstiltskin*, the real version where he tears himself down the middle—and found he preferred the PC mix, in which the little bastard just runs away. What would Gamete have said?

"Gotta realize, Benny," Blince rumbled, slapping a new magazine into the gun, "value's based on rarity, demand

and ease o' replacement." He resumed firing into the panicked crowd—people dropped as predictably as ninepins. "This gun's my pride and joy."

He was referring to a Colt Demograph with a nine inch barrel, which he'd fetched from the squad car as the bank employees began to emerge. It could be set for age, color and wage bracket. Blince had wanted to work in Vegas until he discovered he'd only be allowed to shoot blacks. He liked to throw it wide open. "Why ain't they keepin' still, Benny?"

"Guess it's what they call civil unrest, Chief."

"This ain't civil unrest, Benny, it's civil goddamn insomnia. Pull back. Take out the whole goddamn street."

Everyone reversed up Deal and a Gates gun was trundled forward, steaming like a diesel truck. Denizens froze in its spotlight. Then they were crushed tightly together as though magnetized, and blown to tiny bits. As the cops moved forward, the street was being pelted as if by popcorn. Blince lit a cigar off a burning car and used it to gesture at the blasted bank front. "Now we can begin to find out what happened here."

Rosa felt that if she stopped she'd receive a burn hole, like film in a jammed projector. Pre-detox pale, her face shone out in the gloom of a basement hung with cyberwire and spine X-rays. From here Download ran a sting board full of garbage as a honeytrap for the brotherhood—peeping cops would find their accounts abruptly devoid of cash. Moving cautiously through to the main chamber, gun already drawn, she saw two rocking gyrospheres. Download Jones was bent over a keyboard, hacking frantically, stress-free as a rabbi playing Twister with a psycho.

At the creak of leather, Jones spun to stare, glaucous-eyed.

Rosa raised the gun. "See you after the recession."

When the trigger was squeezed an area of eighty cubic yards was mapped into an ethigraph grid, converging the vibes so intensely that the piece responded only to the needy. The gun was silent. Rosa frowned, suspecting a jam—then knew what it meant. The rounds weren't meant for Download, who'd clunked to his knees and seemed about to sob.

Rosa took a closer look at the figures rolling in the VR spheres like hamsters in a wheel. One was big and one was small. It wasn't Dante and the Kid. It was Chief Henry Blince and Benny the Trooper.

4. IN HIS TENDER YEARS

In his tender years, Eddie Gamete wrote a mindmauler on "The Difficulty of Locomotion on the Upper Lattice Face of a Proton Pulse Bridge." The difficulty alluded to was the fact that Proton Pulse Bridges were a figment of Gamete's imagination and anyone attempting to loco-mote on one would surely die. "And I'll certainly laugh," he concluded.

As he strode across the non-existent landscape, Blince's reasoning was impregnable. No civilian would have been fooled. The brotherhood, however, was trained to disre-gard detail. If anything, Blince felt more secure than ever in the mutable blur of the unreal.

Benny, however, was undergoing squirly symptoms from three hours' circumstance abuse. There were two ideas tilting at each other across the blank, blizzarding wastes of his psyche. The first was that the gunshot limp he'd endured for eight years had disappeared as though he were placing no real pressure on the leg. The second was that Blince was a bullnecked idiot for deeming to leave a geek basement a few hours back without arresting the geek. The VR enhancer drugs Download had hit them with as soon as they entered the basement were neither here nor there. Ironically, Benny's mind was more lucid now than it had ever been, but the clarity was as fleeting for him as for any new inmate or cop recruit. Confronting the lie was so painful he had to believe it to ease the strain.

"Do the Germans have a word for *blitzkrieg*, Benny? It's been naggin' me since we left the cop den."

"We're on itchy ground here, Chief," squeaked Benny uncertainly.

"Do my shell-like ears deceive me, Benny? Skittish at a brace o' cadavers? I'll have you know better than I do—" and he gestured to the bodies around the bank entrance, "these folks are in a better place."

"Some of 'em are maybe burnin' in hell, Chief."

"What did I just say."

The sky flickered.

"And why are you so goddamn edgy?" added Blince as they hit the edit. The evidence of their senses fitzed and sputtered, shorting into a vertigo vortex of TV static. The two cops were almost at the point of thinking for themselves when the scene cut in again—they were back on solid illusion.

The bank stood before them, undamaged and empty of corpses. Any modifications had been voided by the restart. In place of the smoked bulletproof glass of the Highrise was the cheap whiteness of styrofoam. There was no cop backup in the street behind them and the street was unblemished by name or crater.

There was a longterm kickback to the Mall's 24-hour

loop. The theory was that the lack of any lasting consequence would maintain the dull ache of disempowerment familiar from the outer world, but here the absence of effect was so immediate even slabheads perceived it and felt a sense of carefree surrender at no longer having to delude themselves on the issue. The instant the new day kicked in Blince received a deafening volley of laughter in his right ear—he and Benny were surrounded by some of the most savage louts to have slid whooping down the bell curve. The bastards in question took unblushing advantage of Blince's surprise and Benny's distress. Unrelieved years of polychrome abjection turned to hard fury and hit the cops like a diamond anvil. Splinters of panic broke out of the sky.

Blince registered the situation with a flummer of his pixilated jowls and, in a sluggish attempt to pull in the reins, began shooting people for all he was worth. Every gunflash was like a fluorescence bomb and knocked the target to crimson pieces. The broad sweep of his firearm took in bomb zombies, pandemonials and others who had deemed morality a woefully inadequate protection against the modern world. Better guttural cries and stabbing daggers than a shapeless apprehension, thought Blince. "But our concrete actions are unequal to the ideas we hold," he bellowed aside.

Benny heard nothing above his own screams and fired his snub gun with less and less discretion, unreality muffling the reverb. A gridgirl with what appeared to be a sawed-off belly gun put a salvo in his direction and exploded like a doll stuffed with meat. The street ran with berserkers and sim flames of rubine red. He was dazzled by strobe light.

Blince caught a glimpse of Benny being bundled into a cartoon car which roared off, flattening rioters. The bodies were as viscous as a Dali watch, sticking like gum to

Blince's boots. Running, he thought about bugs and their external skeleton. Charmless but happy. People meanwhile buried their bones as deep inside as was physically possible. What were the creeps trying to hide?

Smoking a shock absorber, twitching once for each nerve in his body and speaking artlessly from a technocrazed heart, Download laid out the scam. He'd hacked the Mall less than twenty-four hours ago and had been preparing to shoot up with a jolt gun when the cops bellied in. Jones tendered a dozen rounds at the intruders, who objected reedily while subsiding to the floor. "Admit it— you liked it," Jones had sniggered as he strapped them semiconscious into the VR rigs, the most convenient fixture of restraint. Then it occurred to him to goggle the cops and open the Mall. The more he thought about it, the more suspect and enjoyable the notion seemed.

This was Jones all over. There's a story concerning Download and the slabhead Brute Parker which illustrates the Jones rip. Parker had owned the all-night gun shop on the corner of Dive and when it was burned to a shadow by the cops he attempted to wreak vengeance upon the downtown cop den and everyone in it. The heartfelt plan went awry and Parker went freelance as a hitman. His clients ranged from the IRS to the mob. On one occasion the oil industry hired him to kill the inventor of a car which was fueled by depression. The moguls didn't know how to profit from such a cheap and abundant resource. After ventilating the inventor Parker went to bomb the depression-fueled car as per contract, but couldn't resist trying it out. Due to the boneshattering rage he expressed at the drop of a hat he hadn't enough depression to fill a bird's ear—the motor whined but never caught. Parker torched the target's house but towed the vehicle home and brought in Download to take a look. It was a drophead Spider with a biofeedback net, four wheel drive and a wetware graft engine. Download retuned the graft net for anger and ignorance in a split-propulsion system. Anger ran the front wheels and ignorance the rear. Strapped in, Parker found himself start-stopping like a learner, the rear and front bidding for control. He was thrown repeatedly against the dash, his anger and confusion fueling the process in the most vicious of circles. Jones pedaled alongside on a tricycle, braying with laughter and shouting that Parker could stop the car by feeling a sense of calm. Parker was over the state line before seeing that rather than transcend his stupidity and rage, all he need do was synchronize them. It had been the formula for complacent brutality since the year dot. In a moment of rare gratitude, Parker drew off his mirror shades, uncovering the gun-metal grey of his eyes. That was enough to convince Download he should never sell used eggs again.

But finding himself with two cops in a VR deck, he knew the dry seed of wisdom was dead. He jacked Blince and his yes man into the Mall hoping they'd meet some old friends.

Once in the layout, they made for the bank and Download started to sweat. Though based on Beerlight, the Mall was entirely lacking in detail, which he had to patch in on the run. When they reached the bank he superimposed the sim he'd created for the heist rehearsal, including demographic glyphs for bank personnel. Beyond this he was newted for ideas and, figuring the cops were here about the heist anyhow, lassoed the fly-by-wire in Rosa's jetfoil, bringing her in. "So it's hacker shit," she said now, having heard the sob story. "Freedom in cyberspace'd be fine and dandy if we happened to live there."

"Don't speak ill of the drip-fed," said Download, trying to be forceful through a snot-cemented nose. "Some of the all-time headmen are inside. Babyface Terrier. Billy Panacea."

"We're on itchy ground here, Chief," said the little cop in the sphere.

"Billy who?" asked Rosa, looking for a real steamer. She was sick of fair guns and metabolics—Download's Glock was irreversibly modified for mood amendment. Glancing in a cupboard, she found a microwave pistol jerry-built from a cell phone.

"Burglar extraordinaire. Burgled up a storm a decade ago."

Rosa found a wedge of six-hour ego patches and applied two, stuffing the rest in her jacket. "Listen Jones, I misjudged you—you're not dishonest, just stupid. I brought the wrong kinda gun."

"Count your blessed chickens, Rosa—I nearly flipped my fang when the prefabs burst in." As well as the hand-buzzers surgically implanted under his palmskin, Jones had a toggle under the first right premolar of his upper jaw linked to a scatterat bomb in his chest. "I could have come to a forensically sticky end."

"But our concrete actions are unequal to the ideas we hold," yelled the big cop.

"How 'bout them?" asked Rosa. "They come here clean?" She patted down the nightmaring cops and pulled a Beretta 9mm off the small guy. She slotted the snub into the Approach holster. "These clenchers musta heard about the heist on the way in here—they wouldn'ta got to the scene in time anyway and meanwhile thanks to you Danny's waitin' for the pickup. It'll be no bed o' cherries on that roof."

"Somethin' the nature o' which I may dimly comprehend in the fullness o' time," called the big cop, and the crimewires sniggered despite each other. Download's face, which usually looked as if it had been thrown together in the dark, was fleetingly natural.

A clank of the monroe grill warned of the brotherhood's approach and Rosa drew the snub in time to break four cops like paintbombs against a wall. There was a rear exit and Rosa took it as shots burst off and Download shielded his machinery. Pursued through an underground garage and onto the street, Rosa pelted across traffic into blur-stains of exhaust and neon. Male cops were taught it was okay to shoot a woman in the back, but most still considered this too much of a commitment.

Blince scuttled down a blank reproduction of Scanner Street. Luminescent steam rose from the gratings like a wraith, flickered out, then repeated in an identical pattern. Sodium lights bleached the skullfront of what should have been Britomart and the Vein Arcade. The pagoda roof of Otomo's Needle Bar was like a crude white plaster cast. Blince slowed with a cancering apprehension. He felt as welcome here as a dog at a dance marathon. Did dogs really need eyebrows? he thought. Didn't those mothers know when to quit?

A low thrumming filled the non-air above his head. The street held onto the walls as if a bomb was going to drop. A giant bug was whirring out of the digital sky. Blince made a face and began to run for the mouth of an alley, covered by a flitting halftone shadow. Crashing through clean trash, he looked back—a towering chrome grasshopper with hydraulic rodlegs came to rest outside the alley opening and lowered a head like a jack-o'-lantern, peering in at him with a solar eye of poured steel. A headcap flipped and sprung a rotary cannon full of ammo and surprises.

Blince saw diversity as a disease and never embraced it. He took one swatch at the mischief engine's jeweled thorax and raised his Colt. "I'm Chief Henry Blince. My soul magnifies the law. I'm arrestin' you for incitin' something the nature o' which I may dimly comprehend in the fullness o' time."

The Demograph blooped like a mudbubble—didn't have a setting for insects.

An alternator winked in the armor face.

The bug was an inmate who'd changed her identity code, a hack to get her through the day. And she couldn't believe her luck. Ten years ago she'd been falsely convicted on Blince's word. Imprisoned by a maze of irrefutable conjecture, she'd come to believe that the trials of this and the actual world were rooted in the delay of Blince's death. If this delay were foreshortened or eliminated, the way forward would be crystal clear.

Blince watched the texture-mapped machine's lung inflate and shrivel like a surgical bladder, its gunsighter ranging like the pupil of an eye, the head lock in. His mind too stunned to connect, he saw the cannonfire leap and was instantly looking at Download's cop-filled basement, the afterimage of doom blooming on his retina. A geek in jestware was being worked over with a cable hook. The cavalry had arrived.

Eyephones hung off Blince's face like novelty eyes on springs. The enhancer drug cleared like a nightmare as he reached repeatedly for a gun which didn't exist. Here in actuality there was no such thing as a demographic firearm—the nearest equivalent was the Nafta gun, which killed Mexicans first. As Benny would learn and Blince would never let himself discover, the panicking Jones had armed the cops with copies of the first gun he'd blundered upon in the Mall layout—a virus created by an inmate.

The responsible party was Billy Panacea, burglar extraordinaire, and back in the Mall he was stood atop a virtual building spectating the sad frustration of the bug. It was clawing into the alley mouth like a cat at a rat hole.

When the Blince and Benny borgs popped into the Mall it was the first time in four years Panacea had glimpsed the true enemy. He sat down, turned to the ersatz sky, and knew that in a honeycomb bunker somewhere, his real eyes wept at the hours and years wasted circumventing the interference of the law.

5. IT OCCURRED

It occurred to Dante that midnight in the Mall might not coincide with midnight in the outer world. Waiting had proved nothing. Disarmed by an enormous sense of unreality, he felt more and more complacent about their position. He gazed out of the window, his thoughts dispersing harmlessly. *Am I under the influence?* he wondered. He'd once seen a wave weapon in action. During a little riot in McKenna Square, a cop flung a crucifixion bomb, which skittered into the plaza. A hemisonic flux affecting the guilt centers of the brain converted the entire crowd to Catholicism. Unable to look each other in the eye, the inhibited mob were fish in a barrel for the brotherhood, who slaughtered them before they could lapse.

The cops on Deal Street seemed inert and bored. A few fired at the entrance and bankfront, and someone returned a little. A couple of carshells burned. A mail truck, leadlined against electro-radiation, lay on its roof and smoldered like charcoal. There was a snack stand and situation van.

Dante turned back to watch Corey the Teller reason with the Kid. Trying to buck his ideas up, she was inadvertently undermining the cowardice, laziness, and force of habit which had kept his wrists closed for years.

An escaped braincut subject, the Kid was neurally bonded to his gun. When he pressed the trigger he got an instant flash of his victim's eye view and the barrel of his own firearm. Several convicts had been given the Kafkacell implant experimentally, but rather than inhibit firing it sent them on a kill frenzy, their only motive a repeatedly frustrated urge to self-destruction. The Kid also found it improved his aim.

The heist was mining a rich seam of gloom in the Kid. Lacking the perversity so pivotal to the present headcrime, he was racing to waste. Looking as sad and creepy as a pickled alien, he whispered he'd give a medal to the man who could loosen the iron grip of his life. Corey, who had boosted eighty thousand smackers from the register in the confusion of the heist, considered him her ticket. She would have berated him anyway in her professional capacity as a stranger. "You'd be surprised how sullen *I* can be," she told him. "But you look like a bile fish for Christ's sake. It's wrong."

"Why, miss—what happens."

"*Morally* wrong. Whatever shitstorm of motives brought you here they better be good enough to get y'out."

"Circular thought's a way of surrounding something," he said in a voice devoid of all emphasis.

"What? What are you, nuts? A maniac? Don't you know there's a streetful of army cops outside this doll brothel? Speak up you sonofabitch."

She barked at Dante. "Hey, Lofty." But Dante was reading a book and did not reply. What sort of a holdup was this?

The Kid swallowed a Coma Plus and almost inaudibly stated the view that humanity's demise was rooted in an evolutionary strand which caused its asscheeks to undergo binary fission like amoeba under a microscope. "Every hundred thousand years, miss. First one buttock, now two, in a few years four, then eight, sixteen and so on. And you know where that'll lead. Cumbersome, dragging heaps of dough."

Corey breathed deep a while. A commotion of slaying echoed from outside. That Danny guy looked as hypnotized as a Sega brat. They were surrounded by inflatable bastards. She wasn't any virtual puppet, but this wasn't any virtual heist, so the peril level was even stevens. She'd have to take charge. "Kid. You and me get outta here we're happy as pups in a sidecar. Tell ya a secret." And she drew up a pantleg on an ankle-holstered Hitachi 20-gauge, one of the countless untraceable one-off guns designed on desktop since the Crime Bill. "Life's a geology of precaution. Your pal's knee-deep in himself. You hold up a place without thinking? What if everyone acted that way?"

The Kid found he agreed with the argument—it was what had stopped him from becoming a doctor. What if everyone became a doctor? Who'd drive the buses? By some imperceptible transition he found himself feeling interested. He harbored a sly respect for her leg, the gun and the pink painkiller of her mouth.

Seeing a brawl in a bar, Download Jones had called the cops and been arrested for obstructing justice. A little blister of a crime, it had swelled into pranksterism. Pretty soon he was selling other people to science and slapping fire-eaters on the back so they'd gulp and explode. Now he was sat in a yelling-cell at the end of a distinguished career and a cop was saying, "You pulled off a strong one, Jones—

Chief still believes there's a gun you can set for niggers."

Snowblind with crass mediocrity, the cops were nettled and grateful at having to work over a small guy who was by their standards weird and clever. Download smiled in deference to their coarse elation. They tore off his coat and released a blizzard of ID cards. Download waded through them, yelling that one of them was authentic. An emphatic man who wore his ignorance like a badge of honor engaged him in a no-nonsense interrogation with a butane torch. Download underwent the surgical assault with a stupefying resilience, relentlessly inhaling and exhaling despite everyone's best efforts. Crestfallen at Download's unyielding integrity, the surgeon asked him about the Mall and snipped at him with a bolt-cutter. Download volunteered nothing but fluids. Blood flooded out in great gushing spurts—nature's way of telling him he was bleeding. The overhead fans churned. Download felt like an individual nerve.

"All the world loves a scamp," said the surgeon, "but in this case we'll make an exception." He dealt Download's skull a blow which turned it into a personalized planetarium.

Dazzlingly incoherent, Download began blurting a confetti of ominous statements. There was a device in his jaw—though his personality was on the net, he'd prefer to preserve the meat version, scars and all. The surgeon looked cross-eyed at his colleagues and made a drilling motion to his temple. Misunderstanding, one went out and returned with a power-drill and a purposeful expression.

Now Download was yammering about another device, one he had to reset every day—if he wasn't free to do so it would unleash itself. He rarely made a noise on the subject as there were people who would kill him if they thought it would cause trouble. "Ten past one, man.

That's my story and I'm sticking to it till I'm a seething heap of bugs."

"That may not be long," the surgeon told him, meaning he had a space reserved on Olympus Dump.

For years it had been assumed that expensive overcrowding would lead the city to establish the cod eye sentence for all offenses or abolish visitation and allow inmates to die and rot in an unofficial capacity. But it occurred in a more roundabout fashion due to some low spark suggesting that lifers could be stored cheaply and easily in bulk cryogenic freezers. When the policy was adopted the entire population went berserk in the hope of being slammed in a fridge and thawed out to a better world. The system was turned off and the powerdown blamed on faulty equipment—technology hadn't advanced enough to keep the inessential alive. The authorities saw that the exercise had been unnecessarily elaborate and that rather than stacking thugs in a freezer they might as well stack them in a landfill. The Dump towered over Beerlight, a lesson to potential lawbreakers that the law was already broken.

Download was pounded to the floor. He moved his arm as though he'd the temerity to protect himself. In what form would his atonement come to fruition? They refused to tell him, feigning bafflement. A fist smashed into his jaw and, with a sound louder than a bomb, the building vaporized so fast a dozen bigots were left falsifying evidence in mid-air.

How many times does a man have to shave, thought Blince, before his chin gets the message? He threw the razor aside and gazed through the tank window. Stubborn horrors passed in darkness. That's how fish stay smooth, he thought—no chin. And birds? No chin, forehead, ears or nose to speak of. Imagine an army of such men. Worse than useless.

"Den's exploded," mentioned the driver without looking back. "It'll be Parker."

"Sure, he's been tryin' to put me under the bridge for years—remember the last one Benny?" Blince reminisced. A Barrett 82 Light Fifty blasted at the denfront, the shooter leaving the rig in the road and screeching off in a customized drophead. Brute Parker thought "passive aggressive" meant shooting someone from a lounger. "Sure, distributin' bullets with a real largesse."

"He'll give you the cod eye, Chief," taunted the driver.

"Not me. Nobody'll get this joker coolin' on a slab—nobody but God in his infinite wisdom." Blince thought about an early Parker attack and Benny getting winged. Few people Parker shot were ever shot again. "Someone's been takin' liberties with democracy, Benny. Democracy in its smartest pants."

Benny sat opposite, his face revealing nothing—not even his eyes.

"Wake up Benny goddammit, am I talkin' to myself here?"

"Sorry, Chief—feelin' daffy."

"Daffy ain't an option, trooper boy—what if we hadn't called backup and wound up stuck in the Mall? We'd be gettin' rid o' crooks only to have 'em spring up again to the crack o' doom." He said it without conscious irony. "Boredom shoulda tipped us off Benny, no gettin' round it."

The tank jerked to a stop and Blince threw the hatch open, lolling out and approaching the cop emplacement through the spackle of gunhits. Benny followed after, skirting bodies and bonfires.

A guy with a face like a spaniel trotted toward Blince. "Damn fine to meet you, Mr. Blince. I've followed your career with astonishment and horror. Never in my wildest nightmares did I expect to shake your hand."

"Foresight'd be a gift in a smarter man," Blince remarked, sailing past the proffered limb and peering at the Deal Street bankfront, where employees were screaming demands and throwing out their dead. A cop earthmover ploughed the corpses aside to allow the free exchange of gunfire. "Get a real sense of déjà vu, eh Benny?"

The spaniel man was shouting through a hailer. "The violence you manifest is compromised by its appearance."

Blince stopped in the act of lighting a cigar. "Just what at the subatomic level was that?"

"Testin' a new strategy uptown, Chief," Benny fidgetted, embarrassed. "Phenomenology."

"Phenomenology my bulgin' ass," roared Blince, lumbering back toward the barricades.

"Throw down the guns—an object is an object only insofar as it may happen to resemble what is in your hands," hailed the spaniel man, breaking off amicably as Blince arrived.

"What's your name, soldier?"

"Tredwell Garnishee."

"*What* did you just say to me?"

"My name, sir."

"His name, he says. That's not a name, Tredwell, it's a stab in the back for the forces o' light. All bets are off. I'm takin' over this investigation. What the hell is this?" Blince snatched a bag from Tredwell. "Trail mix? You got trail mix for a bank job? I oughta slap your droolin' face."

"Give him a little credit for tryin', Chief," Benny pitched in.

"Tryin' what? To poison me? Gemme doughnuts and coffee, Tredwell—and baguettes, Macphersons baguettes, with fish sticks and fries. Gemme pasta. Then wait at the situation van. Gimme the goddamn bullhorn. Get outta here." Blince raised the hailer and gave a deep, ugly laugh. "It's all over bar the shootin', boys. You're countin' ten in Italian."

A meek voice from the bankfront expressed a fear of the beef-witted brotherhood, which was known to arrest guilty and innocent alike with a strange certainty.

Blince drew at his cigar and raised the hailer again. "And you presumed to defend yourselves, right? By God, you take that to the perjury room you'll be voted dead by a panel of experts. We'll put you in the chair and bake you to perfection. And I'll laugh my head off, ha ha ha— think about it."

He handed the hailer to Benny as Tredwell ran up with a tray. "Doughnuts, Mr. Blince?" He scrutinized Blince's face anxiously.

"These from the stand?" asked Blince, biting into one. "If I didn't know better I'd say you and your flunkies were usin' unsweetened dough in these. But of course that couldn't possibly be the case."

Tredwell sniggered uncertainly, his eyes evasive.

Blince stared hard. "You're a waste of hair, Tredwell. You wouldn't make an impression on a goddamn pillow. Get outta here before I rip out your spine and dip it in your eye." Tredwell scampered away. "We've fallen on our feet this time, Benny. Such a poignant exchange o' gunfire is a clarion call to those sworn to shorin' up the chill dream o' justice."

"Right, Chief," said Benny, his voice flat as a dog hit at sixty.

"Eh?" Blince gave Benny his full and frowning attention. "Are we, Benny, or are we not sworn to shorin' up the chill dream o' *justice*?"

Benny's reaction was a heady brew of indifference and neutrality.

"You on line, Benny? Your eyes are as glazed as this doughnut." He shook it in front of Benny as bullets and shrapnel spattered the ground around them. "As this doughnut, Benny."

Benny was absently thinking that the doughnut which Blince held against the night sky resembled a giant blood cell, when its center was pierced by the white lightning of ballistic track. The sight was burned into his cortex like the insignia of some forgotten crusade.

6. IN THE SITUATION VAN

In the situation van, Tredwell Garnishee regarded a carnage strata graph. It had never been easier to be shot in the face with a softnose bullet. Instead of drugs, entire skeletons were being flushed down the john. A lion had escaped from the zoo and been eaten by a kid. An old guy had blinded a traffic cop by spitting out a gallstone. A plane had crash-landed on a porn theater, killing hundreds of lawyers. This very day Beerlight was host to a snipers' convention. Tredwell felt he was at the heart of the issue.

Due to the high rate of chief-strangulation in the uptown precinct and an official inquiry which put it down to "stress and hate," uptown chiefs were now appointed on a monthly rotation from the lower ranks. Tredwell had quickly made the leap of imagination from the real world to one in which he was loved and respected. The guys even had a nickname for him— Choke Chain.

"Let's kill the fatted calf, Benny," said Blince, bellying in. "And tell Bazooka Joe here to lay out the scam."

"It's like this, sir," Tredwell began eagerly.

"I seriously doubt it," rumbled Blince, dropping heavily into a chair.

"The manager didn't show, there's the first odd thing. Then a denizen drove up in a junker just before lockup. We beamed this out of security."

A video scan of the bank floor appeared on a tatty monitor. Tredwell zoomed in on a young disaster in an ANTI CYCLONE T-shirt and froze the image.

"Findlay Taz," Blince nodded. "The Entropy Kid."

"What's he holding?" asked Benny.

"Cod eye forms," said Tredwell.

"And he'll be packin' a Kafka gun—an ammo guzzler. The Kid's an escaped bullethead, Benny. Lives a life o' danger to everyone else. Got a psychosis you could hang your hat on."

"Could be in town for the convention, Chief."

"You're puttin' the cart before the horse has bolted, Benny. I saw the Kid take an Uzi machine pistol to a palm court orchestra. His intelligence will surprise and delight you. Get Specter in here—he's a whipsmart fella."

Benny went out and Blince bit thoughtfully into a pie. "This changes everything. Except me."

Harpoon Specter peed on a fire and felt relieved that he portrayed his trade in a town where justice was a verbal luxury. His lucky stars were tarnished with the thanks of years. A night of tank chasing had ended in his misrepresenting a wealthy gran who had witnessed the brotherhood breaking a kid's neck—denial had reached such a pitch, it was illegal not only to premeditate a crime but to remember it later. Now he took up his briefcase and followed Benny to the situation van for a jaw with Blince and his attendant food-stuffs. Entering, he pulled up a chair and insulted Blince in a degree of detail which did him credit.

"You got a point, Harpo," Blince wheezed, broken up with laughter. "I hate to be the one to say it. Watch this shyster, Benny—he can find evidence where none exists."

"Learned it all from you, Henry," Specter responded. He had a big soul which he sold by the hour. "First time I saw you cavorting with the facts my tears flowed like wine."

"Ever misrepresented the Entropy Kid, Harpo? Cop-on-a-Stick here's tagged him for the entertainment tonight."

"Excuse the interruption," coughed Tredwell Garnishee, who had been trying to engage Blince's attention for several minutes. "But that isn't at all what I've been saying, sir."

Blince stared around at Tredwell as though some immaculate boundary of etiquette had been overstepped.

"Lemme bring you up to speed, Mr. Blince," said Tredwell, blithely adding insult to injury. "This here's the bank floor view ten of your Earth minutes before the Kid entered, and fifteen minutes before lockup. Now take a swatch at the other screen." On a second security screen was a view of the vault room.

Just as Blince was opening his maw to ask what in the wide world of sports they were meant to be seeing, a figure abruptly appeared crouching in front of the vault. "Tape jumped," rumbled Blince.

"The tape isn't faulty sir—look at the time frame as I replay it. Bear in mind also that the tapes of the bank floor and the vault room are synchronized—nobody entered the vault room from the bank floor. On the third screen, we can see the man enter the vault itself and wrench a safe deposit."

"What *is* that?" asked Specter, approaching the screen to peer.

"I guess it's a book," said Tredwell, blushing. "After er ...reading a little he snipped the cameras. And as you can see, this man is not the Entropy Kid."

"Well for god's sake break it to me, Blue Boy—how'd the guy appear outta thin air?" Suspecting the answer would shiver the brittle reed of his reasoning, Blince began instantly to fend it off. "It's a trick or piece of chicanery. Everythin' is, right Benny?"

"I'm feelin' stranger 'n Godzilla's chubby son, Chief," said Benny, his voice slurred. "I think I'm gonna hurl."

"Well go hurl at the gunslingers, Benny—our boys need all the help they can get. And these pasta shells are like magnified rugbugs—get 'em outta here."

Benny slammed out of the van holding his mouth.

"The vault works on a phased time lock, Mr. Blince," Tredwell continued. "I believe the thief created an illegal fold."

"It's a time breach," muttered Specter, squinting at a freeze-frame of the man in black tucking the book into his pants. "And I know this guy."

Benny staggered through a spread of ashes, breathing deeply. Acidic wasps were swarming behind his eyes, his brain being sucked through a straw. He was feeling the urge to go to a distant someplace, with something to achieve.

Beyond the siege scene, the street was freckled with molotov flares and Halloween ribcages. Firefly smithereens warmed his face. The shots and shouts grew distant as Benny approached the hulk of a dying car. It was a yellow cab studded with shielding and railway buffers which hadn't saved it. Bullet-riddled and internally ablaze, the car twinkled like a starry sky.

In a sudden pounding flashback, Benny was bundled into a VR car in the Mall, neon strobing and a voice giving him directions.

Back in the now, he shook the recall from his tolling head. He told himself it was a residual drug effect, an eventuality he'd accepted when he became a cop. He could no longer trust the evidence of his senses.

Benny turned back toward the firing, feeling for his missing gun and trying to remember brotherhood policy. A fundamentalist performance was officially encouraged—it was reasoned that a martyr gave better value than an opiate as it could be used and abused at the same time, while a drug was only abused when you ceased to appreciate it. Or was it the other way around? The idea broke like a bone, hurting and useless.

Thought had given him a nosebleed. Tipping his head back, he saw something happening around the side of the Deal Street Highrise, away from the action. A hatch opened on the fourth floor and something ballooned out against the darkness. Eight Hitlers, three Napoleons and a Mao emerged and began drifting upward like a soap bubble cluster. Suspended beneath them was the Entropy Kid and a cackling woman.

Benny crouched, bending over, then looked up again—the Kid too was laughing, his face a toothful grimace as he ascended and was devoured by the sky. Having been cautioned so often against taking the easy way out, the Kid had left by the window.

"Here's the wire on Mr. Dante Hinton Cubit," Specter announced, scrolling the file. "Nationality—Illinoid. Handicap—white. Religion—fetish orthodox. Weighs in at twenty-five years. Father died in a voting accident. Mother missing, presumed skinned and salted. Cubit skipped to Our Fair State after a personality offense, age of fifteen. Once heard to describe the President as 'something to shoot for.' Lotta youth stuff—into Cockroach Centerfold, metabolics, opposed the abolition of privacy. First local offense at eighteen. Used a replica gun to steal a replica sportscar and experienced a replica of remorse. Term at the state clench."

"Vanilla crime so far, Harpo," spluttered Blince, his face eclipsed by a layer cake. "The suspense is killin' me."

"Got into installation jobs. Fired a high-pressure watercannon at an assembly of throat-singing diabolists, strangled a bulge-eyed trout on the internet, bellowed incendiary nonsense at a cowering nun. Broke into a premises on Chain Street, called the cops and got the occupants arrested for burglary."

"Sure," Blince laughed. "I remember the guy—tall guy, right? And the old folks nearly went to the chair but somethin' got in the way."

"They were your parents, Henry."

"Ah sure, I get it—so what's the rap sheet on this joker? You tellin' me he's some heistmaster out of a sheer blue sky?"

"Well, after he moved out of your folks' place he got heavily into data contraband—facts, Gamete, Wardial, like that. But there ain't much, Henry. Off-on association with gun geek Findlay Taz alias the Entropy Kid. Other known associates—Rosa Control the calibertrix, Hazelwood Restraint the socketeer, Download Jones the digital prankster. Usual bicthoughts—wastebound generation, crime stylist, conception of honor impossible to justify or anatomize. Imagine having a brain like that tucked under your hair."

"Well just pardon me while I knuckle a tear from my eye here," said Blince. "Pounce if I'm outta some arbitrary line Specter, but from what you say this demilout's runnin' hog-wild over creation with no better motive than a gratuitous and luxurious will to do evil."

Specter would have asked Blince to explain the idea in more detail, but knew the idea had no more detail to show. "If you say so, Henry."

"Didn't I? Anyone with a segmented spine could tell you that. Now this guy Danny, bless him, already did time in this distorted metropolis so an installation offense'll have him dumped on Olympus at the nearest and dearest opportunity. And by God I'll make the crime fit the punishment if I have to commit it myself."

"That'll take some spadework," said Tredwell Garnishee, who throughout the rap sheet review had sat in a corner, reading by the light of his unimportance.

Blince glared suddenly, but did not speak.

Specter felt embarrassed at having to address an inferior officer. "With all due respect, er, Tredwell, Cubit's either dead or on the premises, and the video scan caught the guy like a snake swallowing a cow."

"I guess this is tantamount to reason, Mr. Specter, but you yourself admitted this here is a time breach. I guess Cubit would know the dangers of it and take precautions. But seeing as the possibility of time breaches are officially denied you'll need to ventilate whoever survives the procedure before he blabs in the perjury room."

Garnishee returned to the *Parole Violators' Bugle*.

Mind a blur, Specter winged it. "No worries, Henry. In fact we could read the charges as we cuff the guy—he'll top the Dump like a cherry on an angel cake." Brandcuffs were now cop-issue—they were lined with nerve-specific electrodes affecting the temporal lobe and, once secured, convinced the prisoner of his guilt irrespective of his actions. Once he was cuffed, the cops had their man.

"So long as he gets dead I don't care about the prelim-inaries," rumbled Blince, lighting a cigar. "Now let's get out there and plug the leak. Oh and Tredwell?"

Garnishee looked up, expectant.

"You're fired."

7. MR. KRAKEN

Mr. Kraken, the bank's head teller, had not been cut in half like his VR equivalent. But he knew that using mainly civilian firearms, he and his staff didn't stand a chance. The bank floor was black and sticky with blood and the air candied with death.

They had learned to stack their dead inside the entrance to avoid their being ploughed aside by the brotherhood. The five people left were wounded and weak. The bank shrewdly offered a pension but no med-ical. Within this framework profuse bleeding and delir-ium was a luxury few could afford.

Discussing liberty with the brotherhood was like doing math with zeroes, but Kraken had to try.

"They asked for food?" shouted Blince, approaching Benny at the firing line. "Pizza? Fries?" Blince frequently lived like a king by intercepting foodstuffs demanded by raid artists.

"No, Chief."

"So what's holdin' us back—morality? Gimme your guzzler, trooper boy."

"I don't got one, Chief."

"Know what Freud'd say about that, Benny? No god-damn gun?"

"Whattya want with mine, Chief?"

"Specter," Blince bellowed, looking for the lawyer. "Harpo, you're packin' what?"

Specter lay his briefcase on the splinter-glittered ground and flipped the catch, unveiling a tri-part Mag-10 Roadblocker. He handed each part to Blince individually, and by the time Blince was fitting the 22-inch barrel there was knowing laughter all round.

A little figure emerged through the shattered bank entrance and timorously flagged a white sheet of memo paper.

Blince checked the 10-gauge chamber. "You know VR was originally used for strategy rehearsal, Benny?" He raised the gun. Mr. Kraken was rubbed out like a scratch ticket, revealing nothing more valuable than his heart.

Dante didn't hear the shot, nor the subsequent Duvall gun fire explosion. He hadn't heard the Kid's entreaties—rising almost above a whisper—to join him and Corey in their leap off a ledge with an escort of gaseous dictators. The Alice-fall of hypertext had him by the legs and he sat shivering in the recursive redrench of data. He'd struck the goldstack—it was the tastiest crime candy on offer.

What's inside a safe tends to relate to what's outside it. Dante had once believed there was nothing of interest in safes anymore as there was no longer much of interest anywhere. He had dwelt in a world of bland daggerwork and convenience killings. But under the gloss of violence he had a phobia he couldn't fight—the absence of ideas assaulted him, a gnawing torture. After a term for rifle abuse he was released into an unrepentant world where denial was the cardinal activity. Murder, theft, riot—they could not permit it to be true. He went around catching ideas about data contraband and information salvage—it was confusing to everyone who knew him. His justifications were banal and lame. He was banished to the back of the riots.

Escaping to Beerlight, Dante discovered the scene. Almost every heist here was an acknowledged beauty. People thought in broad daylight and crime impresarios circused the state. Dante leapt into life's stream with a coatful of rocks. His psychology was irredeemably modified among absentians, spine addicts, text fetishists and others whose vices were too obscure to be noticed.

Living strategically, he retaliated in advance. Inwardly mobile, he laughed backwards. He earned his paranoia from moment to moment. One of the last activities to be commodified, crime had had more time to innovate and diversify. The glow of that knowledge lit his descent into deep waters.

It was the socketeer Hazelwood Restraint who first told him of the prankster Eddie Gamete. Dante knew about Wardial, Panacea, Betty Criterion and other Beerlighters—some of their crimes were on disc—but Gamete was the main event through being actively data-banned. Gamete seemed to have appeared out of and vanished into nowhere like an Etruscan, and people had begun to consider him a sort of dazzling hoax. In the days before the cops joined the army he was a blight on the leisure of both and attracted accusations of blueprinting crime for the populace. But his books contained no descriptions—only aspersions. The thinking man's Camus, he achieved in his first draft what others attained by years of overwriting. In *Caligari's Garden*, two identical men shave their heads and try to grow a hat, straining to push one out. One dies of a stroke and the other dies of a broken heart. In *Trash Tango*, the human race has become so feeble that the alien invasion of Earth occurs by means of a memo. But the planet is saved when the aliens are found to be allergic to pasta, by now a part of every meal. *A Moment's Peace* is about a steam-driven apostle which demands coal in return for which it dispenses its prejudices. Deserted on a cracked landscape, it swipes stupidly at the air and breaks alone. Gamete's novels swarmed with angst angels and others reacting to illness—both physical and mental—by going one better.

Gamete's detractors pounced on his first nonfiction work, a study of the Eurosmudge which began, "A specter is haunting Europe—the specter of Europe." But *The Virus Museum* filled them with glee. It argued that the only interesting thing about serial killers was their tendency to strike again while the snow-haired gran convicted of their previous abomination was in clench—it spoiled the whole process. When challenged by the press about his empirical stand and the veracity of his facts he remarked, "I don't think my book is far from the truth." The remark was reported as, "I don't think any book is far from the truth."

Gamete set up a news service in which all the facts were true. Subscribers had to pay through the nose but the other networks damned it nevertheless as unfair competition—cost wasn't the issue. Three months later, Gamete made a rare TV appearance and was shot, his head exploding in a puce blur. A week later it was found that Gamete had financed the news service by hacking the cartographic world standard, hijacking the international dateline and using it as a whip to horseride the money market. His exploits had been camouflaged by the chaos following the breakup of states. The continent was briefly reunited in synthetic outrage.

Gamete had always maintained that those who led double lives did so because they could only count that far and this led to speculation among textropists that he'd torn a neat one—they whispered of sightings. Others stammered of a rare work—a pioneer of romtext and interactives, Gamete had left in testament a book nobody could read and live—*The Impossible Plot of Biff Barbanel*. Supposedly the work did everything he'd ever been accused of, an irony dipped in blood. It was a digital puzzle box, a thing of dark beauty with the perfect crime at its axis.

A heist doesn't occur in a bank—it occurs in the heart of the criminal. Dante heard about the Gamete treasure and his heart opened like a spreading gore stain. As data went, this was the true spice.

Following leads from bunker to web to needle bar, he learned more—often from blast-due bomb zombies who grasped his arm and urged him to stick around. The book read the reader and, once attuned, told a tale which kicked off with the reader's current circumstances. The book contained a hemisync oscillator which hypnotized the reader. Somewhere in the book was a doorway. The reader was through the door and lost before he knew it. Here was the ultimate role-playing scenario, a maze attuned precisely to the participant's personality. It was vinyl-bound. It was in a safe box in the Deal Street Bank.

In the bank there really was a safe box registered to "Barbanel." Dante had found his crime, like a long lost brother.

Rosa Control had made him promise not to fire up the book until they were away and clear. But he was only browsing, keying up sub-entries, going deeper. He had found a scene where Biff Barbanel glances at a book called *Punching the Sarge*—by clicking on the title, Dante found he could access the full text of *Sarge*, in which a brilliant mathematician shoots himself with a foam gun and drowns. Shortly before this denouement, a football coach quotes from *The Tangle Hymn*, the text of which Dante accessed with a single click. In *Tangle*, there are numerous references to the fictitious author of *The Think Tank*, in which a bigot burns a copy of *Parashite*, which includes a scene in which a drowsy cleric browses through *Knitting the Ties that Bind*, at the front of which *In Your Dreams* is decorously quoted. *In Your Dreams* includes a reference to *Bloody Rest*, in which someone chews up a page from *After the Future* and flobs it at a passing jogger. Seven hundred levels, each level a different book, each written in the "torrential" style so frowned upon for saving time. It was a sub-entry vortex, processing faster than light.

Near the hub, the hypersubtext bulged like a landfill. Boundaries blurred into a narrative metastream. A character tried to determine the average half-life of a cliché by firing sepulchral pieties through a particle accelerator, but an insulation fault left him contaminated and talking bullshit. A fighter pilot roared abuse into his intercom to prove the ego is unaffected by variations in airspeed velocity. A convict in transit convinced the cop to whom he was handcuffed that the cop was the guiltier man, at which the cop shot him and escaped. Speeding past fireworks of information and overhearing a conversation which described the arting of crime by bringing to it a sense of absolute specificity, Dante plunged into a tale in which he lay injured and jostled in a bodyvan, dead or alive. Fact or fiction? Unreachable, he raced into himself.

The bankfront was burning like an exotic drink. "Hot enough for yuh Harpo?" shouted Blince over the roar. "Rome in the last days, I right? Explains a lot. If Rome wasn't built in a day why's it such a goddamn mess, know what I mean? You trooper boys—get this chestnut gun outta here and hose down the crime scene."

The Duvall gun was backed up and a fire crew moved in as Blince and Specter strolled to the snack stand. "If yuh wanna follow this up, Harpo, we're headin' for the uptown den—Terry Geryon's your man. Main den's been Parkered. Hey, what am I thinkin' here—Benny? Put out an APB on Parker. He'll rue the day he rocketed outta the birth canal. And let's clear it up once and for all Benny, can potatoes only be grown from potatoes?"

"I guess so, Chief," said Benny, itching to be gone.

"You guess," Blince rumbled ominously. "Think you're pretty smart, don't you."

Benny smirked uncertainly.

"Eh?" Blince stared at him. "Think you're charmin' the cats outta their ruby-red pajamas."

"I gotta go put out the all-points, Chief."

"Listen Benny, I don't like this any more than you do—hey!" But Benny had scuttled away. Blince turned to Specter. "This from a guy who wanted to play incidental trumpet for the movies. Make any sense to you?"

"Listen, Henry, about this here bank job—Cubit turns up I wanna misrepresent him. I need a high profile case for the networks. Last one I had was the O'Leary murder, remember? Even the murder was televised and there was no doubt who did it."

"Sure I remember— two-year sentence, right?"

"And that was just the opening remark."

"Sure, but Harpo," said Blince, opening a soda on the vendor's teeth, "I don't want anyone huggin' and relieved in the perjury room. Somebody's gotta top Olympus or there's no resolution."

"It's my job to correct the truth, Henry, and if that requires blinding these here Seceded States, who's to say what. This whole town's the smoking gun of ignorance, after all. We'll receive massive duplicity."

"You mean publicity."

"I guess I do, at that."

The bank had been dampened down and they wandered over to take a swatch.

Inside, Blince swept a floodtorch around the bank floor—every surface was covered in a black tar and his boots made the tack-and-rip sound of velcro as he proceeded to the vault. The air smelled of steak and he began to wish he could get out for a decent meal. As he emptied four beans into the relevant safe box with a trooper snub, Specter appeared at the vault room door.

"It's a neat job."

"Neat as a Swiss roll pushed into a determinedly closed mouth," muttered Blince, taking out the severed hand. "You know they used to cut off the dukes of thieves in the old days?"

"What goes around comes around."

Blince threw the hand back and took out the vinyl-bound thesaurus, scrolling. "Well looky here. Shoot at someone for two hours you think you know 'em. 'Dishonest, unsqueamish, slippery, artful.' This hits the screen we got eight seasons right here."

And right there Specter started to doubt his strategy. Blince's pursuit of retribution was blind—like a marching toy, he had to hit something before he could change directions.

Rejoining the cleanup brigade outside, Specter got a beer and watched a gang of speed urchins swarm over a tank which was stoved into the base of an elevator. Though too poor to interest him, even these brats could recognize a valuable corpse.

Yet when word came through from the data boys that Dante Cubit's ID matched one of the bodies swept away earlier, only Specter and Tredwell Garnishee received the news with a semblance of solemnity—then quit the scene in a screech of spiked tires. Everyone else was swell, and amid fistfights and racist dancing, agreed that the entire affair had been a waste of time.

On the corner of Crane, a bodyvan spun out and plunged into a storefront, the rear doors bursting open to spill the dead like worms from a can. Dante Two crawled away from the corpse heap and lay bleeding in the road. It was what he called his "Italian look." At his belly, the gore-blot spread like a Rorschach butterfly.

Flat out and counting the stars, he wondered at his body's perversity in leaking neither more nor less blood than it had at its disposal. Would Rosa be angry?

PART 2

THE LOOSE END

In the Delayed Reaction Bar on Valentine the fashion cycle had narrowed to a point and revivals of the present moment blended with those of every other moment to make a dead, slate-dark sludge. This sludge was baked dry and sold to fugitives who could not articulate a time when things were different. The clockhands were still and the room spun around, confusing people's aim—ammo ended up in folks who were slow to grasp its value and their unworthiness to receive it. The ballistic jukebox played a perennial favorite as the Entropy Kid and Corey the Teller pushed into the bar—the steady spatter of an Ingram M11 sub.

Once again the barman welcomed the Kid back into the "land of the living." Whatever your strife, Toto knew it to the bone. He had bought the place knowing the trustiest rule of social disintegration: bars burn last.

"Gimme an October Surprise," the Kid whispered.

"I'll have a shake," announced Corey sunnily as Toto spun a mixture of antifreeze and a solution for stripping the velvet from giraffes' antlers.

"Who's the prefab?" Toto asked, switching off the centrifuge, but the Kid stared morosely at the bartop. Contradictions tore at his head—she asked him to open up and was disgusted when he did. She said she didn't want to change him yet wanted him to be happy. She stuck as close as a tattoo. She thought with her hair. The Kid toyed nervously with his gun.

The lights went down for the Migraine Cabaret. Performers came on in lime-green face paint and shuffled slowly about the performance space, closing curtains and lying down. Two merged their checkerfield hallucinations and played chess on the rippling result. The crowd gamely bellowed in bewilderment and impatience.

The lights came up. Corey was still alive.

The Kid's despair had continued like a fire crossing a bridge—to his mind it vaulted a gasoline river anyway. He led a charred life. Action was consumed and futile. Aiming the Kafkacell at himself only shorted the circuit. Aversion surgery prevented his using another weapon. Every suicide line he called turned out to be an anti-suicide line. He was trapped.

"What you get," said Corey, watching him, "tryin' to escape from a clench that don't exist."

"Yeah, things ain't been the same since they clenched Panacea," mused Toto, wiping a glass.

Had anyone ever escaped from the Mall? thought the Kid absently, gulping antifreeze. Not even Billy Panacea, burglar extraordinaire? It'd take outside help.

He remembered his breakout attempts at the braincut unit where he was bonded to the Kafkacell. He and his cellmate, Dice "Killer" Agnew, had disguised themselves as guards and been beaten up during an escape by the other prisoners. Dice got inhuman after surgery, and escaped without him. The Kid awaited contact from outside, but there was zip. All he had was surgeons and guards to complain to. One sympathetic doctor involved him in regression therapy and the Kid discovered seemingly repressed moments of happiness in his childhood, but it was a classic case of false memory syndrome.

"Look behind you, Kid," said Toto.

A clown wearing forensic gloves lugged a rotary cannon from his table and walked out.

"Missed him," said the barman. "That was the Carny. In for the convention."

The Kid was surprised and impressed—as slaughter went, this harliquinade assassin was the true spice. The Carny would scream like a demon as he let fly at motivational speakers, celebrities and diplomats, seeming to shoot from the heart. Nobody could guess what inferno took place in his cosmetic skull.

"Agreed to speak," said the barman. "Quite a coup for the bigots' bunfight."

An idea began a miraculous germination in the baked interior of the Kid's mind. The bartop had begun to whirlpool, creaking.

"Speaking of which," said Toto, "you hear about Download Jones? Blew his gourd—redecorated the den in full and final fashion."

"Cod-eyed?"

"Eyeless—heart of the blast, remember. Brotherhood escorted him backfirst into the den and in two shakes of a lamb's tail, blam—ask round you don't believe me. You know Jones—acutely paraphernaic. Not only that jawtrigger but some kinda virus bomb, supposedly—needs a daily reset. Guess if it's true we'll hear them socketeers a-sobbin'." Toto roared with laughter. "Everyone sayin' Jones hacked the Mall—Blince and his yes man did the bust."

"Cod-eyed?"

"Na. They went to supervise a heist on Deal—big party goin' down there. Regular jamboree. You and Danny still doin' a job there sometime?"

"We just did the job, you son of a bitch—the jamboree you describe is what you get when something fails absolutely, all the way down the line. Smithereens, Toto, that's what's going down in Deal Street—the smithereens of my life, and yours." And he lunged across the bar at Toto's unprotected throat, shaking him like a street mime.

"Ho-ho-hold your horses, Kid—I didn't mean nuthin' by it."

"Yeah, what's got into you?" asked Corey, prying the Kid's hands from the barman. She was just glad nobody had seen them escape, borne aloft by tyrants.

"Sold down the river," whispered the Kid, guzzling the rest of his drink. The heist, that stupid heist which had happened, God help it, for real despite Dante's virtual paranoia, had gone totally to seed and thorn. He reached into both pockets and came up with handfuls of painkillers, which he began popping like beer nuts. He gazed around blearily, images doubling. The graffiti coding on the wall was visually reconfigured, as the artist had intended, to reveal an atomic missile hack.

"Rosa was there," said the barman in slow time. The bar was underwater. Corey's face looked plastic. "Ask the Rose."

Someone selected a burst of Ruger Mark II on the jukebox. There were groans and some violence from the clientele—the Ruger was considered close range, elevator gunfire.

Harpoon Specter entered the Portis Thruway and the maelstrom of his self-regard. The Cubit affair would put his ass on the map. Two versions of the same guy, both guilty of intent but only one guilty of theft. Court TV— one Cubit on the show and the other a surprise witness. He'd skip the brandcuffs, let Cubit yell his head off re the facts—the existence of doppelganger matter created by timefolds, and the annihilation caused when twinned objects met. It had happened once, obliterating a city— Cincinnati as luck would have it—but the authorities attributed the blast to just another private plutonium jag.

What if he could get the two Cubits to hug in Los Angeles, at a post-trial press conference?

Then he remembered that at least one of the Cubits was dead of bullet inhalation. But even with two corpses, couldn't he box them up and send them to the target state with instructions for single-plot burial? There were planting parlors who'd honor it, for twins. Then, boom. The idea was itching like a lifeline in his palm. He'd have to get a rundown on the Deal Street bodytags.

Specter sped out of the Thruway and the mass of Olympus Dump filled the windshield, overshadowing downtown and the Beretta Triangle. At Pill and Crane he hit the brakes—a bodyvan was hunkered down in a storefront. Taking up the Roadblocker, he stepped out and strode across the street. The only other movement was the contradictory flashing of a busted stoplight and its reflection in a bloodslick.

He gave the van the once-over. No Cubit among the bodies. The driver dead, his neck broken. A thesaurus on the ground near the open van doors—Cubit's ballast, version number two. Specter was picking it up when a cop roller slashed to a stop, lights pulsing, and Tredwell Garnishee ducked out with an armored arm rifle. "It's not like that," said Specter before Tredwell had spoken.

"Step away from the vehicle, Mr. Specter."

"Well, well, the nodding dog," said Specter, bringing the Roadblocker to bear. "How are the mighty fallen."

"Fine, thanks. And now I must ask you to drop your steamer and step aside."

"Oh I get it. One more rogue cop in this town? And packing what looks like a fair gun."

"This is a Zero Approach Arm Cannon, Mr. Specter. I have pulled both the trigger and the BOD pin. One false move."

"Benefit of the doubt capability—you have a doubt?"

"No sir. Merely a code of behavior."

Specter stepped slowly away from the van, keeping the shotgun raised. "Boy, to have a code of behavior—how that must feel. Address book resembles a wafer, am I right?"

"Where's Cubit?"

"Curled in a doorway somewhere, bleeding to death. Time's of the essence, Tredwell. That your real name? Somehow it's too distressing to believe."

"No doubt the sack of shadows you call a philosophy spares you the pain of believing anything." A tank taxi sped by and they resisted the urge to look away from each other. "Parallel universes do not meet, Mr. Specter. Or shall we say, they should not be allowed to."

"You understand I've a limited time to stand here being lectured to by some fired semicop with a brain smaller than my fist."

"Duty is in the eye of the beholder."

"I don't mean or need to belittle your career, pro-pellerhead, but Blince assesses people's character by the way they sound falling downstairs. He has a downer on you, and always will. Bring him Cubit, he'll rip off your balls and call you a consultant."

"I don't make the rules."

"Then you're an idiot who needs to cultivate the faculty of manipulation. The trouble with the law is that it's yet to fall into the right hands."

"We can't all have a collateral limb structure, Mr. Specter. Or your low bandwidth morality."

"Fool's gold and fossil fruit, Tredwell—hearsay and heresy. Justice anywhere is a threat to injustice everywhere. If they isolate another Cubit back at that napalmed bank it could work in our favor. Time to grab the snail by the horns."

"You can keep your snail. And your straw man notion of justice, which had its beginnings anyway in the kind of revenge you propose."

"Congratulations—you've spotted your first irony. Tredwell, you're as boring as a self-important movie extra playing a mayor."

"And you are the most depressing excrement to have sluiced through the bilges of history."

"This interchange is useless."

"You are free to fire."

"Wild courage implies the end of all restraint."

"Yes."

Specter head-faked a little and Tredwell's Zero Cannon started buzzing like a wasp swarm. Specter couldn't believe he was being stood off by someone as dynamic as a bigot in a peat bog. Garnishee had previously exhibited a meekness which was difficult to justify and it had unnerved Specter. And now this gush of defiance.

Specter was used to stating his opinions as law, a practice known as Dworking. He'd utilized it in the perjury room to clear a guy who'd shot a hundred people near a gun shop. Citing American military procedure, Specter proved that the slaughter was a pre-emptive strike. Another time he got a total innocent worked up as a multiple killer despite a transglobal alibi—the only doubt was the guy's state of mind. Sanity was denoted by the presence of remorse, but since the accused was innocent he had none—he was deemed as crazy as a chef and thus unequal to the task of knowing anything but evil. As a lie the law had the virtue of being visible. All it took was a little leverage.

"Maybe the Chief'll take you back for this," he said, producing the duplicate thesaurus. "It's the book Cubit boosted. Must be a…rare edition or something special.

Cubit was a textropist, after all. That what you are, Tredwell?"

"Give that to me."

As Garnishee extended his hand, the gun encasing his other arm dipped a fraction. Specter fired and Garnishee's Cannon instantly blasted back.

Rosa stormed past brainstem piercing salons, gaudy needle bars and gore-tarred car wrecks—neon signs flickered and buzzed like rattlesnakes. Alert with anger, she watched details pass with a hypodermic intensity. The microwave pistol felt alive in her hand.

Shouldering her way through a crowd on Dive, she felt strange—Download's ego patches kicking in? Maybe it was near dawn—like many others Rosa had inverted her sleep patterns so that day was night, night was day.

She stopped in front of what had once been Brute Parker's all-night gun shop, now a drill bit fetish emporium. Pretending to examine a 20mm Heavy Duty Impactor, she watched the dark reflection of someone standing still in the crowdflow behind her. The figure pushed quickly forward and she turned, firing the pistol—on a long setting, it passed harmlessly through the crowd and exploded inside a TV store across the street. She struggled to re-range as the Entropy Kid stepped into the striplight, slapped the gun from her hand and whispered hello.

2. PUFFING ON A CUBAN

Puffing on a Cuban shock behind a desk which resembled a steam locomotive, Hustler Meese nested in an underworld basement. On the wall behind him was a tattered poster of Kennedy's erupting head and a "BBs KILL" slogan. Meese got into the murder game when he realized the taking of life was being portrayed as perfectly acceptable. He quit the army with a toy-neat philosophy and an M60 light machine gun.

Meese was debating whether to send a scout to the shooters' shindig when someone banged into the chamber trailing blood like a noir shadow. Parts of the person were black and smoking like volcanic vents. It shambled toward the desk as Meese stopped drawing on the Cuban, his only concession to surprise. The man dropped into the seat opposite.

"Mr. Meese, my name is Tredwell Garnishee."

"I guess that explains it."

"I wish to hire you, Mr. Meese," said Garnishee, his breath grating. "My own efficiency is now impaired."

"You don't say. Who's the target?"

"Mr. Dante Hinton Cubit. Here is a photograph. He is possibly armed, and probably wounded."

"Some party. Sure I can put someone on it. Pulse-collecter. Inhumanity of a saint. Name of Brute Parker. Got a real fascismo about him. Used to run a gun shop. Half bastard, half bastard." Meese exploded with loud, honking laughter. "Only guy I know could shoot someone from the other side a revolving door."

"For special reasons," continued Garnishee with effort, "I wish for Cubit to be completely obliterated. No remains, Mr. Meese, this is the deal."

Meese leaned back in his seat, frowning. "We got a special service for doppelgangers, Mr. Garnishee."

Garnishee's eyes, which had been squeezed shut in pain, sprang open.

"Sure I know about 'em. Couple times a year we have to do one—this town's nicest kept secret. Never knew a loose end I couldn't handle. They're paranoid, insecure, know they don't belong. Surplus to reality. Long as you get the right one."

"Mr. Meese, I am in a dreadful hurry." Garnishee was tilted aside in his seat, beneath which his reflection tilted in a lake of blood. He reached under his scorched coat. "My card."

Meese took the smartcard and swiped it through the machine. "This won't take a minute. Um...Where was the target last seen?"

"Crane...Street."

"This won't take a minute," Meese repeated, staring at the machine.

There was an extended silence, punctuated only by the faint *pat* of dripping liquid. Then Garnishee coughed horribly, his body wracked. The machine began to whir at last.

"We're in business." Meese tore off the slip and placed it before Garnishee, holding out a pen. "Sign on the line."

Garnishee, drained by the gargantuan effort to see beyond his eyelashes, directed the dregs of life energy toward his hand. He clenched the pen in a fist and brought it to bear like a crayon, trying to recall his own signature. He tortuously signed as though forging a stranger's name, then dropped the pen.

"Here's your card," said Meese, "and here's your receipt."

But Garnishee didn't take either. After a moment, Meese reached for the phone.

In a hideout off a subway inspection tunnel, Brute Parker was systematically fieldstripping his mind. A spartan psychology made it a quick task. He began again. A buzz alarm alerted him to someone's approach and he put aside a big word issue of *Throatknife* which included details of the sniper AGM. Straddling a wooden chair and swivelling an XL73E2 Light Support Weapon toward the door, Parker thought of the changes time had wrought on the bloody mayhem industry. The old three-day cool-off period had enabled customers to plan ahead—it was a boon to those who knew themselves well enough to predict their next rage. Nowadays, nobody ordered in advance. Shithead protocol had given way to bastard fatigue and stupid, arty guns. Drug guns, fax guns, fossil guns, wetware guns, anabolics, guns which fired calories, guns which charmed the birds out of the trees, static electricity guns you rubbed on your sweater, microsoft guns which fired an hour after the trigger was pulled, glark guns which did something surprisingly different each time, deconstruction guns which turned everything to shit.

Parker was in demand as a hitman because he had principles. When he heard people scream during an attack he said they were speaking with their "true voice." He knew he was making an impression on someone when they started coughing up blood. The higher the caliber the higher the contrast between the target's health before and after being shot. Never wear beige. He lived by these rules because he had made them. They made him the elite in a scene flooded with amateurs.

"Conventions," he rumbled.

Dante Cubit appeared on the security screen, and knocked the special knock. Parker released the door.

Dante Two had always based his choice of pants on whether they made good tourniquet material. So when he entered the bargain surgery dive on Scanner he was pretty tidy. In fact, despite everything he was feeling better than he had in years. So what if he was superfluous? He didn't feel superfluous. And wasn't everyone, under a certain wage level?

He was thinking of Rosa, his cock ticking like a bomb. An aching, intravenous beauty, all crucifix earrings and cracked tarmac leather. He saw her spread upon a bed of liquid codeine, grinning from head to toe. She was wired so differently it hurt.

These considerations kept him strong under the knife, holding little pains like trophies. He intended to live until death forced him to abandon it.

His coat and guzzlers had been boosted by those who took him for cod-eyed. Now at Parker's door, numb with painstunners, he anticipated with relish the thrumming energy which coarsed in a fine gun or blade. Parker's armory was the full rip.

The door opened onto the barrel of a bullpup machine gun.

"This is what I live to see," Dante Two laughed. "A guy who is generous and liberal in matters which are inevitable."

Dante Two's statement peppered the wall over Parker's head but, seeing that Dante was alone and unarmed, Parker stepped from behind the XL Light. "You wanna guzzler, Danny Cubit?" And he stood utterly still so that the alloy gleam of the rifle racks drew Dante's eye.

All of fundamentalist Christian life was here. Armalites, Remingtons, Weatherbys, Webleys, Ingram subs, Uzi barkers, Hecklers, Redhawks, Bulldogs, Streetsweepers, Mossbergs, Bloopers, Caliburns, Macs and Mitsubishis. No roids or metabolics. There was what appeared to be a blowpipe missile in the corner. Dante Two waded through flechettes and shok lock rounds.

Beautiful antiques. A stainless Smith & Wesson 659,

packing fourteen 9mm rounds into a staggered line box magazine. A Steyr 5.56mm AUG with a cycle rate of 650 rpm and grenade capability. A Remington 870 riot gun. Dante Two was in such a good mood he cracked a joke about Parker's "antipersonnel ears." The only flicker of response in Parker's expression was that of the striplights reflected in his mirror shades. Dante Two cleared his throat and became deadly serious. "This Beretta 92F now Parker, what's the charm velocity?"

"Fully 1,280 feet per second, Danny Cubit. Modified to a twenty magazine."

"I need a steamer which would disencourage the brotherhood from approaching an edgy fugitive wanted for a crime he has not achieved."

"The H & K Tolerance is your man, Danny Cubit. 9,000 foot-pounds and 3,000 fps of charm." Parker lugged a semiautomatic minicannon from the wall. It was pupstocked, had a 30-round mag and weighed 25 pounds. A gridpulse replaced the sighter. "Muzzle break reduces recoil by 30 percent. I have placed my heart and soul carefully into this machine, Danny Cubit."

Four years ago the Intolerance Gun had been doing the rounds, but the joke was on everyone. A variation on the Stone Pistol—which instead of aiming at the target ignored everything the target wasn't—the new gun dealt with the target by going into denial. But it was clear to the denizens of Beerlight that intolerance of a target didn't make it go away—at best only sent it underground a few years.

As a believer in gun karma, Parker shunned the Zero Approach and its like. Fair guns automated judgment and took the responsibility out of the user's hands—he considered this immoral.

But there was something about the new gun which

appealed to him—a potential for the most direct expression of contemptuous disregard. He set about engineering the fatally dismissive in the postbyte age. With the help of his scareweather friend, Download Jones, he reversed the ethigraph grid codes. Rather than acknowledge and reject the target the modified weapon never recognized the target at all—this was utterly annihilated by the force of the shooter's ignorance. Energy was conserved by scorning the need for a reasoned rebuttal. "Tolerance" was a shooters' abbreviation.

"I'll take it," said Dante Two, delighted. He paid from the discreet surgical cavity in his forearm.

After his departure, the phone rang and Parker picked up. Hustler Meese from the rub out agency. "Got a commission—a jim-dandy. Client died right here in the office—the boys just took him away. Evaporation job—guy called Cubit."

Parker slammed the phone and holstered a Scatterat as he banged out of the hideout.

Dante Two was swanning down Link sprouting his worth—he felt he could take on the withering world. The sun peeped over the horizon like a timid sniper.

Two headlights opened out of the dead mouth of a subway entrance and a black drophead roared onto the street, shrieking to a stop. Brute Parker stood out, aiming an Ithaca 40 Scatteratomic. Dante Two bolted as the wall behind him powdered, disappearing. He concluded that Parker had had a change of heart. It must have been that crack about his ears.

"Doesn't sound like the Danny I know," muttered Rosa as the Kid got through describing Dante's weird inertia after the heist. The Dante she knew was so unreserved he meditated dressed as a rocket. Why hadn't he left with these morons?

Rosa lived in a shipwrecked railroad car off the Loop Expressway. It was just like a trailer home except that it didn't explode when you turned on the gas. You could sit in one chair and see anyone approaching from either side. It was the kind of place Santa Claus would live if he was a Mexican.

The Kid drove them up in a car so hot it came with a serving suggestion. Rosa unlocked and immediately discarded the micropistol and empty cop snub. The place was filled with gaskets, pill bottles and other obtainium. Corey lowered herself gingerly into a leather jawseat. There were leather curtains and a leather alarm clock—maybe it woke you by creaking.

The Kid sat bored as Rosa peeled apart her antishocks and washed at the sink. A slash of light glinted the armorblasting flechettes with which her nipples were pierced—she swizzled them like cherry-sticks, a daily ritual to prevent them bonding in. "Jesus," Corey whispered.

"What else Toto say at the bar?" Rosa asked, noticing the sodden ego patches on her arms and tearing them away. Her mind fuzzed and straightened out again as she blinked.

"Download had a reset rip," sighed the Kid. "Posthumous revenge virus, I guess. Twenty-four hour timer."

"Let that slide," said Rosa, replacing her armor. "Since you don't know what snaffled back there and Download's oblonged, we oughta face with Hazelwood Restraint before makin' a move."

"That surface-to-air failure? He ain't the full dime."

"He can talk to Download's download and monitor the copnet while he's ported." Rosa hooked up a Sauer 226, a Dartwall .33 and a slimline street sweeper, this last in a thigh holster. "And anyway he was in on the heist at the seed stage, right?"

"But no matter which way he's facin' his hair points to the magnetic north pole. And a fat lotta good that'll do us."

"Don't drag me into your accuracy, Kid—you're all wrist, you know that?" Rosa glanced at Corey. "Comfortable, honey?" Then she opened what Corey had taken to be the fridge. Inside was a bubbling perspex tank, in which something like a furled manta ray hung suspended. Waterlight rippled on its mottled surface and a bladdersac swelled and subsided. Rosa tapped the glass. "Gotta replace the nutrient suspension—there's sediment."

She opened the top of the cooler and dunked her right arm to the elbow. The wetware gun wrapped around the limb, sealing itself to her seamlessly. Rosa tensed as though armwrestling, was pulled off balance a little, then gradually relaxed. She drew her arm out of the tank, swaddled in biomorphic datamuscle. It was like an arm cannon, but interfaced with her nerveweb directly. The gun had a pulse.

"It," Corey stammered hoarsely, barely audible. Her eyes were big as hubcaps. "It's dripping."

"Let's get moving, Kid. Sun's up—streets'll be empty."

Hazelwood Restraint was a serial innocent whose mind had grown too big for his head and spilled into his heart. He went off on tangents so extended they met the tangents of Martians coming the other way. The kind of tall that seemed to be dangling from a meat hook, he appeared constantly surprised at his own clothing. Even his shades seemed involuntary—he'd stop and tear them off, staring at them in bewilderment. Anyone who was anyone avoided him like the plague.

They found him in the Safety Net, a jolt bar on Snuff Street. Antidudes, glum and menaced, pretended not to look at Rosa's tits and arsenal. The last out, she turned at the door and fired a volley into the gloom.

Restraint's place was a brittle apartment off Valentine, and he welcomed them with outstretched arms as they pushed him inside. He turned on a lamp and checked the bug traps, saying he'd discovered the cockroaches were motorized. A magnifying glass showed up the mechanism, disguised as twiggy meat. "And that's all she wrote," he shrugged, and popped a beer. He used the can to gesture at an elephant foot TV. "Don't worry," he said, "it's not from an elephant—it's a diseased appliance." Leaving the room, he returned with a pillow which he rustled, saying it contained seven hundred thousand ant beaks.

"Let's get out of here," the Kid whispered.

"Hazelwood," Rosa announced, "I hope for your sake you make our presence here worthwhile."

"Or I leave months later in a pulp sack, right?" beamed Restraint, nodding like a Pez. "That a squidgun, Rosa? Hey, I bet you would."

Rosa assented quietly.

The lamp threw Restraint's rocking shadow on the ceiling as the three inquisitors sat on the couch. "Danny Cubit," Rosa began.

"Cubit—oh boy, I've been growing tusks trying to figure him out. Here's what I've come up with. Due to a cosmic administrative blunder, the human race has been given the wrong planet to live on, so we can never quite get comfortable. This means—"

Rosa cut in with a news flash on the heist disaster.

Restraint had been insulated from these facts by a postfuturist introaction which would have appalled Lovelace and other figures of classical cybernetics. People had discovered with delight how to kill socketeers—plug an electric guitar directly into their head jack and hit any chord. "A heist of the mind—wow—Danny was demanding trouble with that extravagant plan of his." Restraint shook his head, grave and grinning. "Years walking round full of crimebabies, and when it was finally his time—biggest anticlimax since the turn of the century."

"Trope-on-a-rope here still reckons Download sold us out."

"It was the free decision of our sonically-challenged friend to co-top the heist. Crime is as irreversible as an egg, children. And you were tooling with data contraband, where the truth can be revealed by the tug of a light cord. Too casual, you wake up in a bombed giftstore."

"What in hell do you think you're saying?" whispered the Kid, standing and flagging his arms. Corey sat clenched in the certainty of impending violence. "The bird's been at your brain tissue!" It was known that Restraint had lost an eye in a belly-laugh accident and used the socket as a bolthole for a wren he had nursed to health.

"Say again?" asked Restraint, smiling.

"We wanna rip any refs to Danny on the dredge," Rosa explained, holding the Kid in check by the throat. "And talk to Download."

"You're barking along the wrong lines, Rosa," smiled Restraint, rocking back and forth on his heels. "Every bit of this so-called robbery feeds into Eddie Gamete. You think if the rumors were true he'd leave his treasure in a vault made of macaroni? Lemme read you something by the man." He took down a copy of *Planned Reaction Utterly Redundant*, a showcase of ten American NWO strategy backfires, starting with the 1990 Haiti election. He recited like a cafe poet brought to life:

Surgeons expecting to find the soul by hacking people up repeatedly rejected the existence of their own by their behavior—only the respectful might be allowed a glimpse and these never defiled the body. Compare this immaculate safety device with the lessons offered freely and ignored. A crime archaeologist recently excavated a heist preserved in the Pompei lava flow. The crook is aiming a spear at a shopkeeper, who is loading loaves into a bag. The shopkeeper's expression is no less or more surprised than those of today in similar circumstances—nothing has been learned in the intervening years.

During the recitation Corey had been squinting to identify an object which rested on a side table. As her eyes grew accustomed to the gloom, she became convinced that it was a smooth perspex replica of Abe Lincoln's disastrous beard.

"Gamete," Restraint continued, "said any act worth a damn could not be ignored, and when an effective person is ignored it's the result of a deliberate series of steps on his or her part. Children, I now have proof that these ribs of mine are furled insect legs awaiting my command to spread and scuttle. Watch me now." And he began breathing heavily from the diaphragm.

This was a red rag to the Kid, who steamed headfirst at Restraint and rammed him to the floor, punching. The shadow of their flailing arms darted back and forth across the walls. Restraint's shades flew off and the wren shot out of his socket, twittering crazily around the lamp.

"That's it," said Corey, standing, and walked resolutely out despite her knowledge that in this part of town she'd get a cab with a photo of the devil on the dash. Behind her she heard Restraint screaming emergency landing instructions in an unnecessarily Scottish accent.

Benny turfed one of the databoys off the den system—the earlier talk of Billy Panacea had led him to review the files. A dozen pre-Dump escapes from the state pen with the aid of his mother. Posed for an aura photo which resulted in a monotone mugshot and arrest card. Stole gravitons from a dozing bishop, who had to be bagged down from the ceiling with an eel net. Benny was halfway through the file when he realized there hadn't been any talk of Panacea earlier. Why was he researching Panacea?

"Keepin' up with old friends, eh Benny?"

Benny spun to confront Blince, who stood gnashing a hot dog the size of a barrage balloon. "Bitta background work, Chief."

"Goddammit Benny you been chewin' air since we got the call on that hacker—I wish to God we ignored it and went straight to Deal. Don't you know or care Billy Panacea's outta our jurisdiction? He's in the Mall for an outta-state job stealin' guard dogs. Did an entire sweep o' the new state o' Terminal and sold 'em to the city pound. You're wastin' jacktime on a dead case and I'm plum angry."

"Guess I got interested, Chief."

"There ain't nuthin' in Terminal territory of interest to us, trooper boy. You wouldn't catch me gettin' caught stealin' guard dogs in that neck o' the world. Law without farce is indolent, says Pascal, and you know what that means in a state that ain't even halfway Pentagon-aligned." It was the custom in Terminal to punish some as an enticement to others. Fame by injustice was derided by those who attempted to smash upward by force of criminality. Yet to Blince, the only inherent value in apprehending the real culprit was that he'd be easier to frame. "I came here to order an APB on the Entropy Kid—corpse ain't been identified at the flashpoint. And I want the timecrime secure file—somethin' about this whole pastrami-on-rye I don't understand. And Benny, your obsession with that has-been sonofabitch Billy Panacea, burglar extraordinaire, is jeopardizin' my entire digestive system. It's throwin' a spaniel in the works and I'm orderin' you to put your face to the pedal."

"Don't I get to exercise some intuition, Chief?"

"Not while I'm around," said Blince, and walked out.

There were a quarter million copies of Download Jones's personality on the regulated dredge and offweb, but when Restraint ported he recalled that he'd never met a mind-model construct he liked. Jones's download was more poignantly inadequate than most. PC in a PC, it lacked life-urge, mischief, humor—all the sparks thrown off when a soul meets a body. Jones had released these squigglers for the sole purpose of baiting dredge users from a preprogrammed taunt stock. Against the greyswarming backspace revolved the Jones icon, a crimson monkey head with chattering ivory teeth. "The Master," said the download, referring to Jones, "used the same data in the virtual walkthrough of the Deal Highrise as is contained in the official city schematic. This act doesn't conform to the criteria for the practical joke you describe. You are sexually inadequate—this is why you socialize with machines."

"You were copied four years ago—you wouldn't have this prank in your memory."

"I include no plans for the future—the Master deselected them during the scan process—his pranks wouldn't function if every net user knew of them in advance. You dredge-heads are so amazingly effectual you can be silenced by the dimmest Neanderthal wielding a rock."

"What about the original safe version at Jones's place, the mainframe?"

"It may contain such information—neither I nor any other copy has ever communicated with it. You sad bastard—this is your whole life."

"And the reset virus, what is it?"

"It may be a prank—I know nothing about it. Get a job you pathetic—"

Restraint jacked out and related his discoveries to Rosa and the Kid. "Scan for any refs to Danny," Rosa told him.

Restraint searched. "A Cubit ref a couple hours ago in tandem with a smartcard receipt—Meese Agency, a stoppage outfit under Tinder." Rosa was already out the door and gone when Restraint added, "And correspondence on the copdredge—a rap sheet transfer, and confirmation that he's cod-eyed and on the way to Olympus in a body-van. You just popped in too, Kid—an all-points. Lotta shit about the Mall hack—everyone saying it's the first time in years they haven't been bored rigid. And that's all she wrote." Restraint unported, looking around. "Where's the Rose?"

The Kid was trying on the perspex beard. "I think the necessity of being dead increases," he whispered.

Corey the Teller stood on Dive, the epicenter of the Beretta Triangle, and watched a pasty-faced guy mime the further unfolding of his ear. Then he funneled his hand against it and listened with exaggeration. Clearly astonished by what he had heard, he began to bend-walk on the spot. Corey pulled her Hitachi pistol and put the guy down with one shot. Right there was what she hated about this neighborhood.

Straight off she regretted it. Out of Saints Street sauntered a dozen deathers with ill-matching hardfloor guns, alerted by the pistol crack. They got a fix on her and started down the street. She fired five times when they were too far off, dropping two. The others began running toward her. She put her last round into the downed mime and turned to flee.

And came face to face with a gaunt, grinning wreck. "An accident isn't the opposite of anything," he said, his teeth clenched—gripped between them was a ringpull. Corey looked down at the grenade in his palm. Bomb zombie.

An armored car screeched up, its door flung open. Corey got in and slammed as the vehicle blasted off. "Need a ride," said the driver without inflection—behind them the zombie had his moment, the explosion blunting the edge of a corner block. The car hit the deathers without slowing, wipers smearing the window gore into arcs. The driver threw a switch and the hood flipped over, levelling a row of rocket bloopers. "How far you going," he said tonelessly.

Corey looked at this little guy, his eyes set on the road, and glanced around the car's interior—the floor and seats were littered with take-out trash, drug bags, ammo and snuff magazines. Corey felt suddenly nervous of the boosted eighty large in her pants. "You a cop?" she asked the driver carefully.

"My name's Benny," said Benny. "But they call me... Benny."

"You found time to shoot Galt the Finger yet?" shouted Meese into the phone, then realized there was someone standing in his office. "I'll call you back." He hung up as a vision in newsurvivalist antishocks stepped into the light. He knew who this was—a shootist he'd wanted on his books for years. The Rose, with her wraparound dark side. Meese hoped his mental adjustments were externally undetectable.

Rosa Control seated herself opposite. Meese's mouth slithered into a smile. "Miss Control. Can I do somethin' for you, or are you offerin' your services to me today?"

He waited for the Rose to ask what he had in mind. When she didn't he continued for a while, talking shop. ". . . And Webley never made a more charming weapon. I'll have you know as well as I do. Better."

Rosa studied the growth-inhibited, steel-plated nails of her left hand.

"So," Meese struggled. "You goin' to the convention?"

Rosa raised her right arm and leveled the wetware gun at Meese. "Are you beginning to see what I mean?"

Meese's face turned white, then the bright blue of new denim.

"Call off the hit or I sponge the wall with your brain."

"Oh the," said Meese, watching the gun breathe. "The Cubit hit, yeah? I just, Miss Control, I just wonder if you know how difficult that is, see even normally, but this is Parker's hit—Brute Parker, understand?"

"How endlessly interesting."

"Hey now listen," shouted Meese, offended and angry. "You try stoppin' him once he's off—threatenin' Parker's like threatenin' a bomb. And this here's a double hunt."

"Explain."

"It pays high 'cause there's more at stake. Hell, the whole town'll blow if one of them Cubits don't get evaporated."

"So they're both still alive. Who staked the hit."

"Guy by the name of Tredwell Garnishee."

"Don't play games with me, Mr. Meese."

"I'm tellin' you that was the guy's name. Drop the squidgun, Rose. The hitter's out, I can't stop him. This is hard for me too—you think this is easy for me?"

"Your ease is a matter of indifference to me. Pick up the phone." Meese picked it up, watching her warily. "Contact Parker."

"You won't shoot me, lady."

"Prove it."

Meese dialed a number and Rosa fired, hitting off the crest of his head. He regarded the ceiling in astonishment, the air aswirl with blood pollen.

Rosa took the phone from Meese's hand and listened to the gunsel on the line—it wasn't Parker. Parker never took calls while out on a job.

She put up the phone and walked around the desk to swatch Meese's data files—what she found made her question her perceptions. The desk was filled solid with meat, an extension of Meese's body attached by a bundled ganglia of gristle. The wooden exterior of the desk existed solely to conceal this flaw in his personality.

In the Deal Street Highrise, his face uplit by dataflow, Dante experienced the hunting of Dante Two. He could see from his lateral vantage that the Tolerance gun was a toy against Parker, who was utterly indifferent to external acknowledgment. The question of whether Dante could warn him, whether Dante Two was himself, whether this was fact or fiction, never germinated from a seed in his mind. If Dante Two was shot in the laughing gear, it was mere logistics.

Dante was unaware of the figure standing in a corner of the warehouse, arms folded, watching him.

Don Toto the barman shoved the final felon onto the street and closed the Reaction for the day. He'd had to give a mime a haymaker to the belly earlier for the fool's own protection. The clientele had been appalled by the mime's reaction to the blow—not a sound, just an exaggeratedly glum expression and those cowing eyes. The last he'd seen of him he'd been walking against the wind in the direction of Dive.

Toto extinguished a small fire, stacked the seats on the tables and swept away a few spent shells. The ballistic jukebox had broken down again, encouraging the clientele to provide their own deafening amusement. Walking to the rear wall, Toto detached the jukebox front and knelt at the works with a nerve-jumper. An entire junction of the circuitboard's fuses were corroded. He tested a strip with the needle and the jukebox exploded with Sauer fire. The idea was to isolate which selections were still available and which were lost—the latter were causing a shutdown when selected.

The next tweak of the board seemed to produce a deafening explosion and a kind of animal yell as, behind him, the door to the Reaction evaporated and Dante Two skidded inside on his belly. Frowning, Toto hit the circuit again to produce what he could have sworn was a blast from a Scatterat—an Ithaca 40? He rejumped the point—Ithaca for sure. Then here was something sounding like a misfiring Tolerance gun, segueing with a sort of yell of despair. He'd had no idea these selections were available.

Parker stood in the doorway rapid-firing the Scatterat as Dante Two ditched the useless Tolerance and dove over the bar to raid Toto's riot response gear. Parker had overturned a table and ducked behind it when Dante Two, standing from behind the bar with a .44 Harry Magnum in one hand and a Redhawk in the other, blasted away with both. Parker discarded an empty Rat clip and pulled a flatline flechette gun to cover the reload. The table was being bitten down like a cookie.

"Technology," thought Toto. The circuitpoint which had just provoked Scatterat fire now produced a mix of two .44 Mag stoppers and the shriek of some kind of flatsuit barb pistol—making zero sense. He needed a hardware troubleshooter like Download Jones. Then he remembered Jones was cod-eyed in the cop den rubble. Boy, Parker would thank him for that.

Toto scraped at the component as though removing lead from a statuette. The air ignited with ballistics.

Dante Two was standing on the bar tilting at Parker, who stood suddenly with the reloaded Scatterat and fired, blowing the bar out from under him. Every single glass in the Bar exploded as Dante Two rolled and hit the doorway, bolting out. Parker followed, letting rip. Toto stood, threw down the nerver in disgust, and turned to the wasteland of his establishment.

Specter's cell phone went off as he entered the Triangle, but since he had lost an arm to Tredwell he had to stop the car to answer it. His secretary informed him his entire legal staff had been flattened in some kind of aircraft disaster. Specter was an expert in fractal litigation, whereby the flapping of a butterfly's wings on one side of the world resulted in a massive compensation claim on the other. Somebody would pay.

He looked down Aphex Street, empty. He wasn't telling Blince this, but he knew Dante Cubit, had misrepresented him when he was a mere underwolf. It was a personality offense—you could catch ideas just by looking at the guy. This was in Chicago, where Specter had been waiting on a few forged papers. He'd tried to demonstrate to the court that Illinois was packed full of individuals—this meant coaching a number of witnesses in isolation for a fortnight. Sick as dogs, they reedily requested TV privileges and, when refused, withdrew into media starvation coma. Specter had to inject a second group with a choline-arcalion centrophenoxine hydergine piracetam ID-frame booster chased with milacemide grail speed. An hour after the drug was administered the witnesses began to sneer, saying if Specter thought they were sticking round here for a lousy grand a day he was off his lid—then they punched his face, each taking turns to do this, then neigh with laughter while prancing out of the perjury room. A mistrial was only averted by Specter's instantly pulling a revolver and leveling it at his own bonce while standing side-on to the jury and chirping, "Brains in your lap? It ain't pretty!" The case continued until Specter lost it due to a show of childish petulance, during which he pelted the judge with sewage. Dante was convicted, and slipped custody disguised as an escaped criminal.

Specter thought fondly of the days when he'd tear off the eyebrow of a witness and blow it toward the jury like the seed-head of a dandelion. Where were those days now? And where was the money in those days?

He felt for the cybersurgical porting stump at his left shoulder. After the Tredwell encounter he'd called his red phone surgeon on Orbit Heights and been fixed up with an autograft arm of undifferentiated reptile tissue.

This was designed to inhabit the etheric after-image of the missing tissue and fill it out, fleshing the ghost limb. It flowed into the damaged form and whatever was absent was speedily replaced.

Maybe Specter's man did it as a joke but no ethical surgeon would have given fillerflesh to a lawyer. Specter opened the case on the passenger seat, removed the limb, unsealed one end of its transparent packaging as per instruction, opened the port valve at his shoulder and applied the arm—alert to absence and tendrilling in search of the vacuum to be filled, the reptilian presence streamed immediately into his soul.

Dante Two ran into Aphex Street, a gutted grey thoroughfare parked with a single armored executive car—as he sprinted past this, he became wired with recognition. Parker skidded around the corner to see his quarry standing, staring at a stud car. Wary and suspicious, he approached the figure and brought his gun to bear. Then he saw that Harpoon Specter sat in the car, convulsing.

Specter's left arm was a rippling cylinder of guacamole, and a similar substance was squirting out of his ears. He was yelling incendiary abuse which was inaudible to Dante Two and Parker as they stood in frank appreciation of Specter's performance, their concerns forgotten. This was what Dante Two loved about this neighborhood— catching up on old associates and seeing what they were doing. For Parker's part, he knew that whatever Specter was up to, there must be money in it.

Then the two spectators glanced at each other, remembered the full weight of their differences, and resumed hostilities while bolting in the direction of Olympus Dump.

At the same moment, Benny and Corey blasted through the border checkpoint and roared into Terminal State.

5 . MEANWHILE

Meanwhile, the media had detected the rudiments of the heist on Deal. Diligently shaky news footage showed cops laughing fit to burst amid wreckage. Handball Weyrich, Mayhem Correspondent for the *Daily Denial*, commented that "the bank never seemed so unintimidating as after the fire storm hit. There was an air of celebration uptown as one of Beerlight's oldest traditions was upheld." The Mayor took swift action with his arms and lower jaw as he said, "Nothing but a fundamental change will prevent these acts of animosity. Let us forget the past—this is the only way to be genuinely surprised." From an armed airship circling the globe, Leon Wardial the technobooster remarked that the heist showed great promise—the perpetrator had created an expensive mess which was not a mere "artifact" of decadent aesthetics, but a true reflection of the city's nature. Pat Logan agreed: "It blends so perfectly it may as well never have happened. I'd be surprised if this wasn't simply the camouflage for a more interesting crime."

Henry Blince skimmed these last remarks in the *Parole Violators' Bugle* while eating hot dogs at the counter of the Nimble Maniac. "Hey Dobey!" he yelled. Dobey came out of the back. "Dobey—gimme *another* hot dog!"

"You had enough, Chief," said Dobey, shaking his head slowly.

"What I gotta do to get some service round here,

admit a mistake? I'll know from the *bottom o' my heart* when I had enough—now gimme another."

"Okay Mister Blince, but from here on into eternity I ain't acceptin' the consequences."

"I ain't offerin' you the consequences, fryboy, just a few smackers squeezed outta the rock o' this state's economy—right here." He smacked the cash onto the counter. "Y'accept cash from a cop, am I right, fryboy?"

Blince returned to the *Bugle* and Logan's thoughts on the Deal installation. "One is left with the impression of a stage, dressed and lit, while the action is proceeding behind the backdrop." Blince snorted—the *Bugle* was scrawled by a bunch of banjo-playing timewasters who didn't know which bucket the head was under. "Bunny-huggin' liberals," he rumbled, then rolled the paper and rammed it down the throat of a crumb-awaiting dog.

The classified time breach file was more compelling. Seemed Specter and maybe even the dancing chimp he fired knew more than they'd let on. The brotherhood had escalated internal cover-ups after the crime strike embarrassment four years ago—the only people conspicuously unaware of the strike were the cops, who had gone on killing and looting as usual. Time breaches were worse because they affected property on a grand scale. There was a quote from a Professor Guppy:

Many theorists, God help them, had believed that a subject who pranced backward in time would cease to exist when the timefold had elapsed, the naturally time-bound version subsisting. When, under lab conditions, time was first folded back it was found that the subject who had traveled backward, and the version of himself occupying the past naturally, both subsisted beyond the experiment's duration. The time traveler was molecularly volatile, bone idle, did not belong and knew it, exhibiting a darling paranoia and disassociation. If left, the time-travel subject deteriorated over a span of days, becoming increasingly dangerous due to this molecular volatility. Worse, it was found that the slightest physical contact between the two versions of the subject resulted in an exquisitely violent molecular event. It was clear that both versions could not safely be allowed to persist—the time-traveler must be incinerated at the nearest and dearest opportunity. The other, it must be stated, was as happy as a dog in a sidecar.

It said here Cincinatti was the result of some guy experimenting in a garage—time got folded over and there were two versions of the same guy. One fainted and the other tried giving him the kiss of life, destroying the city in seconds. It was the sort of scenario Cincinatti folk had always dreaded.

Deal was shaping up to be worthy of Blince's attention. And he started to wonder, did eels contain caffeine? Maybe just the head, which was the only possible reason for chefs to remove it. "Hey Dobey, what happened to them hot dogs? They ain't out here in one minute, I'll rip off your ears and use 'em as suckers to climb that wall over there—right there."

Blince's radio went off—they had a lead on Parker.

When Dobey emerged with a fresh stack, the eatery was empty. He began sobbing like a child.

Restraint and the Kid picked over the trash in Jones's digital foundry. They'd passed the stripped skeleton of Rosa's jetfoil in a side alley—the only major component remaining was the rotar hub, because the brotherhood had clamped it. "This is hardsoft heaven, Trope," said Restraint now, punching out a safe door's lock spindle with an airhammer. Download's mainframe was linked to the offweb by a one-way airlock cable and for some reason was electron shielded. Once inside, there was an old-fashioned screen and keyboard.

This first generation download took a swatch at the schematic of the Deal Highrise now on the dredge and compared it with a version of the city plans stored in its memory. "Quite different," it stated. "And I haven't been revised since my inception seven years back. The original schematic relates apparently to a multi-level stealth fortress. The official city plans have been hacked and amended."

"That's that," whispered the Kid. "Download thought he was onto the right stuff but someone had messed with it. And that's what newted the heist." The Kid began idly sifting through a heap of prankware. He turned up a few clowny masks and, under a polkadot flak jacket, a scooby rifle. In front of a boarded-up elevator stood a medicine locker.

Restraint asked the download about Jones's reset virus. "No information. But I doubt the Master would seed a virus which would decimate his own download constructs."

"But you ain't affected by the dredge, am I right?"

The medicine locker was stacked with drug clips. The Kid selected a cocktail cartridge and started breaking open the others, filling the cocktail clip with grail wizz and IQ boosters.

"I'm not affected by anything—nor do I affect anything."

"So what's the point?"

"Running a system is the quickest, shortest, and only sure method of discerning emergent structures in it."

At the shot, Restraint fumbled the keyboard and

turned to see the Kid with a jolt gun aimed at his heart. Metabolics were unaffected by his aversion program and as he sat waiting for the cocktail patch to dissolve and the intelligence to come on, his pupils were the size of wrecking balls.

Restraint couldn't believe the brotherhood had left so much jolt gear on the premises and gave silent thanks to a gummy god of his own invention. "All dependence and renunciation go unrewarded," he said, inspecting the patch clips, "in the universal jaws of experience." He found more works under a floor panel near the gyrospheres. "Ramone," he gasped, addressing the bird behind his shades, "we've hit the paymother." One eye wept and the other sang.

The Kid had seated himself at the keyboard and begun a lightning inquiry. "What am I worth?"

"Value is based on rarity, demand and ease of replacement."

"It depends who you ask?"

"Precisely. A friend would say one thing—a cop, army, or business another."

"So what's the point?"

"Running a system is the quickest, shortest, and only sure method of discerning emergent structures in it."

The Kid booted out and closed the cover on the machine.

"God's speed, Kid," called Restraint. "But more care." When the Kid left, Restraint was priming a syringe the size of a clarinet.

Parker's bigotry-propelled car was a short way from the subway entrance where he'd abandoned it. Numerous strip-heads and speed urchins had tried to boost it and only got a few halting yards before the motor cut out.

Soon after, a few cops had given it a try, but none had got the balance right. Blince squeezed inside and the car glided smoothly off, disappearing into the haze of morning bonfires.

Dante Two couldn't keep his mind on the chase, no matter how much he told himself it was important. The details of the day struck him harder than any bullet. Sunlight glinted off a Subaru sign, rust brittled an oil can, kids kicked through the smoke-plume ashes of the dead, Olympus threw a shadow over hordes of muggers addicted to Mace. This was surely the most lurid of worlds and he had never felt so much a part of it. The Dump's wire fence hove into view and Dante Two recalled a nursery rhyme from his Chicago youth:

April in the breaker's yard
Yes, my arms are very hard
Rub them every day with lard
April in the breaker's yard.

He was bent over laughing, when above his head a window splintered outward and the sound of mirth and light machine gun fire escaped from a second story. Costello—he'd recognize the Mexican's calibration anywhere.

Dante Two entered the building and, racing up the stairwell, plunged into a sniper's party. Everywhere he looked there were frenzied tableaux of impromptu torture and freestyle garroting. The mildest of discourse was punctuated with the chirping flight of daggers. Old and trusty friends improved the shining hour by punching each other into the middle of next week. The bewildering tangle of alliances was decipherable only by the frequency and angle at which wounds were inflicted. The entire crew had staggered from the Tree Museum to Deserters to the Delayed Reaction, and were weeping old tears. At one end of the room was a giant cake housing a naked and drugged senator.

On a couch sat Costello, discussing dialist subcontinuism and drinking a Reaction takeout entitled Counterfeit Reality Strain. He called Dante Two over for support. Costello had been given six months for crucifying a Valley girl and everyone was boasting that if they'd been allotted that much time they could have crucified fifty. Now he belied his exopose by discussing the annihilative dangers of attempting to purify a thing which consisted entirely of impurities. "I've given this town the blood-heavy shirt off my back," he said in disgust. "And that's the long con of existence here—police and thieves, eh? If they don't got the spirit they oughta get outta the quivering meat wheel, Danny. Outta the goddamn loop. The city's the bad guy. Help yourself to cloakers, my friend."

On a coffee table was a large bowl of anodyne pills, used to damp down original thought and reduce conspicuity in public. The practical hazards of reexamining one's mental premises on the wing were well known to the denizens of Beerlight—a guy skyjacking a plane one time had pushed a gun to the pilot's face and instead of demanding a flight to Cuba, snarled, "The cultural space vacated by logic and morality has been filled at once with an automated and meaningless simulacrum which is nevertheless of precisely the same dimensions." A kidnapper started assembling a ransom note from scissored headline letters and finished a year and forty thousand words later with the words, "and won't accept the jig's up even when faced with a show of apathy equal to their own." The kid he kidnapped had long since escaped. Another sparkhead entered a bank right after a romantic breakup and delivered a bitter monologue on how "women send signals but men speak English" while performing the most mawkish heist in Beerlight history. He later wrote and signed a confession which, published under the title *The Seahorse's Gaze*, replied to theories of gender manipulation with those of hermaphroditic self-fertility and indifference.

Some denizens would mix anodynes with smarts and watch everything gain and lose meaning, need it and not give a damn. The very walls pulsed in a fast alternation which made cloaker-smart cocktails a fashionable substitute for rave strobes. Those who could afford strobes and pills practiced the art of intersecting the two elements by synchronizing and desynchronizing the strobe frequencies to provoke a series of profundity pile-ups or empty vistas—depending on whether you were tuned in.

Dante Two wondered if he should have downed a few cloakers before the Deal heist. He'd agreed with himself that if he entered the bank to find he was the second Dante on the scene he'd allow the time-tripper to ventilate him. A necessary sacrifice. But he hadn't gotten rebellious—he'd followed through and didn't feel in any way guilty for surviving the shot. In any case he'd felt weird about dumbing out, even as a disguise.

"We are acting much too well, and procrastinating," Costello told Dante Two, staring him in the eye with his fist. "Digitizing guns as if we cannot trust our own senses. Look at this." He picked up an AMA Long Range Rifle. "Thirty-four pounds of dismissal, my friend. Fired by you or me it has a meaning. Computer-assisted it's merely a movie. Carry on that way, we end up on the stinking dump out there. Take it from me, Costello Ignore Anaya."

The party started breaking up to attend the Convention, which was kicking off around now. Dante Two said thanks but no thanks, thinking about Rosa. He loved her from the black ice of her boots to the pink icing of her brain. If she were blown to pieces he'd love the pieces. He headed out.

6. RESTRAINT

Restraint had stupidly volunteered to provide an amusement at the snipers' rip—he'd got a degree of notoriety for his performances at the Delayed Reaction. "I spy," he'd announce, "with my little eye, something beginning with T." Then he'd release Ramone the wren, who would pluck the wallet of a bleary onlooker and return it to Restraint amid applause. "Theft," Restraint would explain, tossing the wallet back, empty. But he found the audience would bellow guesses regardless: "tree," "trampoline," "turtle," and be genuinely baffled at his consequent rage.

Today he had something different planned. When he was a kid his mother had always tried to stop him picking his nose by saying, "God can see you when you pick your nose." This guarantee had led him to create a snot graffiti which said, YOU FUCKED UP BIG TIME. But in adulthood it occurred to him that maybe God couldn't read. The thing needed to be simpler.

So now he stood on stage before an assembly of rivet-eyed mercenaries and picked his nose, backed by a fast-cutting projection of starvation, death and disease. The worse for Jones's joltware, he began laughing and performing a strange, jerking dance. He had forgotten the purpose of the exercise, and the MC's introduction of the piece as "Mister Restraint and his Amazing Eye" put the cherry on the audience's indignation. Small arms fire began cracking out from various points in the auditorium—it was impossible to tell from where. Restraint was clutching his arm, then his leg, and then dragged himself from the stage, the back projection continuing.

Elsewhere in the McKenna Square Assembly Hall, the Magic Bullet Contest was again cause for dispute, due to "unfair use of technology" such as radio-guided smart projectiles, as participants tried to reproduce the Oswald shot. Ted Jellicoe's popular session, "Awaken Your Inner Lout," competed with the knockabout seminar on "Pointblank Gunfire for Fun and Profit," given by Jonah Dervish. The main screening room was host to heist shows—in exasperation at the poor quality of surveillance footage, criminals had begun shooting their own exploits with top-of-the-range equipment. Shootists argued over the source of the quote on the program cover: "A sniper is like a genius—it's not enough to be one, you have to be one *at* something." Delegates' bags were bomb-checked on the way out of the building.

Minor stars were present—Hammy Roadstud, Dino Harmaline, Early Del Mar, Ted Revenant, Addison Fenway, Leo Struction, Mena Whitewash, Hillary Clambar, Craw Duke, Sally the Gat, Belly the Whump, Rex Camp, the Caere Twins, Sam "Sam" Bleaker as the mindless violence representative for the mob, and Heseltine Finn the cokehead, who appeared on "Wanted" posters as a blur with eyes. Finn's image had resulted in the repeated arrest of Marzipan Chad, who was famous for his ability to spontaneously generate a digital anonymity blob over his face. Chad was here to confront Finn and a fight had broken out between the two indistinct figures. Trying to pry them apart was Chewy Endeavor, a guy so into the notion of a second skin that he'd had his skin removed and his musculoskeleton bound in leather, then his own skin restored on top. Unanchored and bloodless, the human skin had soon worn away and left him a creaking leatherman.

But the big star was the Carny, exterminating clown extraordinaire—and he was in a broom cupboard, bound and gagged with emergency cordon tape.

Dante Two approached his apartment building. His car, the Smokebelch, was still concealed behind trash in the alley. Entering his apartment, he found everything in place. He removed the Eschaton rifle from its wall cavity and loaded up, making a list in his mind.

1. Leave town by east side and circle.
2. Hit the airport from north side.
3. Boost jetfoil.
4. Locate Rosa and Dante in Alaska by rumor trail regarding damn near impossible sexual escapades.
5. Claim supremacy over Dante in mindbendingly cunning chess games which last for months, evenly-matched Dantes guessing each other's moves to a T.
6. In the fifth month, have Dante kidnapped and subjected to a course of neuro-linguistic self-improvement which actually alters his submodalities and thereby his very personality. Thus faced with an unequally adjusted Dante at the chessboard, don a boxing glove and punch his lights out.
7. Seal Dante in indestructible floating arboretum fitted with world library and riches beyond imagining, wherein his every thirst may be satisfied. Set perfect environment adrift in Bering Strait, disguised as iceberg.
8. Reconsummate love for Rosa in quarter-mile jacuzzi brimming with priceless dinosaur DNA and broadcast images via satellite mirror onto dome of White House.
9. Release a macro virus which changes everyone's

name to Mickey Dolenz, wrecking the tax system. Declare the western hemisphere the Dolenz Free Lands and set up a new multipartite democracy in which charm and nervous tension prance hand in hand through the meadows, blinding one and all with the beauty of life.

10. Crown self with replica of universe formed by ozone sky-lens focusing ten years' cumulative focal data down 3200-mile refraction shaft into earth's core, solidifying image in pure magma diamond a meter thick. Declare that all is well and all shall be well. Explode.

He had pocketed a handful of anodyne cloakers at the party and now swallowed them in preparation for the ramble. Then he stuck a kingsize ego patch over his belly wound and sat there wondering why the room hadn't ignited. All this stuff belonged to Dante, didn't it? And Dante Two was a fugitive from reality. What was on TV?

This last thought informed Dante Two that the anodynes had kicked in, halving his IQ. He primed the Eschaton and left the apartment, diligently repeating the list in his mind.

1. Take the time to say a long good-bye to everybody. Take a final look at those landmarks. Don't get a ticket driving that car.

2. If pursued by cops, nearly collide with fruit truck, causing it to shed its load across street.

3. Mount sidewalk for no reason and plough through dozens of trash cans.

4. While driving, have a shave in preparation for mercy-begging.

5. If windscreen smashed by gunfire, run car into storefront.

6. Drop gun.

7. Run down blind alley, stumbling over dozens of trash cans.

8. Hit tall wire fence and clamber frantically upward.

9. Mindlessly climb fire escape to roof, wrestle on edge and fall, landing amid dozens of trash cans.

10. If arrested, call attorney—more expensive the better!

When Olympus Dump was fifteen stories high, they built a ski slope over the bodies. It was decreed both pleasant and educational for denizens to skim down the bleak decline. Rosa Control passed through the Dump perimeter by the toll booth entrance, leaving the money-taker with his future round his ankles. She skirted the Dump, kicking through rats and birds, a ski mask shrouding her against clouds of flies and effluvia.

The wetware rifle started to throb as she approached the Dump's front gate from behind—this was where the dead were checked in. About to press the rifle to the back of the sentry's head, she was surprised when he turned and put the prow of a Mag-10 shotgun against her forehead. "Think of it," he said. "For just a few years the dead were finally a minority—now this." He tossed a glance at the Dump. "Let's go."

They started up the slope, sliding. "He's not on the register, Miss Control. You here to dig up Danny or to bury him?"

"Bury him."

"I don't believe you, Miss Control."

Gulls exploded upward with applauding wings. Rags of stuck flesh flapped from Rosa's boots.

"Very swank gun, Rosa. Look at this." They stopped on a plateau and she looked around at him—he was flexing his left arm, which glistened like the skin of a snake. "It's like a drug."

"But can it shoot?" asked Rosa, and continued up the slope before he had replied.

Toward the peak the Dump surface was mainly bare bone, picked clean and smooth as ice. Rib cages caved under the climbers' weight. Chalky powder became the order of the day. At the summit, Rosa turned to see Specter holding a patchy head. "It's Jerry Earl," he said. Grey soup spilled out of the skullbowl. "I defended him on the rap he got here for." And he smiled like a gashed throat.

"Why are we up here, dickwad."

Specter ditched the head. He went and leant against the rear of the ski hut, then gestured with the Road-blocker. "Take a swatch at the city, Miss Control."

Calculating the moment to shoot, Rosa gazed over gutted blocks, little fires and sparse insect cars on the distant freeway.

"Look at the dupes—the husk of reality they work to finance and which they spend their leisure hours believing. Oppression evolves."

"I hope your monologue evolves beyond the obvious."

"Now don't make a scene. This crass menace is just the traditional prelude to a shot in the back around here."

"That's old style murder, Mr. Specter."

Specter stepped toward her. "Isn't it though."

But when she spun to shoot, Specter already stood with his hands in the air, the Roadblocker on the bleached ground. Brute Parker had a slimline armani gun trained at the lawyer's smile. "You shouldn't oughta shoot a lady in the back, Harpoon Specter."

"I didn't, did I?" asked the lawyer.

"I don't like you," stated the hitman, his face expressionless.

"Well you can see I'm real choked up about it," Specter remarked as Rosa pitched his rifle into the abyss.

"You wearin' beige pants," stated Parker.

"You looking for Cubit too?"

"Tell me what you know about that."

"Not a Lazarite hope, Parker. In this boomtime for horror the cost of clarity's a burden no one can afford. Tell you what though. You answer a simple question, I consider it." He held up four fingers. "How many fingers I holding up?"

Parker shot one away. "Three."

7. THE BIG ACT

The big act had the main auditorium filling to the brim as the previous speaker wound down. "...And have demonstrated beyond a doubt that as an outlet for snipers capitalism has been indistinguishable from the agrarian commune. Thank you." To barely polite applause the speaker departed the lectern and, after a pause, another figure strode on, swaddled in clownwear. The attendant snipers greeted the Carny with respectful applause.

Keyed up on smarts, the Entropy Kid whipped off a jester mask he'd boosted from Jones's basement and, speaking in a strong, clear voice, addressed the assembly with a level of audacity and charm rarely endured in this neck of the world.

"Yes, it was I, all this time, who fooled every bastard here by dressing up as a clown. And why. By god, you can ask? Where's the evangelical carnage that made this city the mayhem capital of America? Where are the nervy programs of priceless pandemonium we used to take for granted? Where are the Panaceas, Diesels, Atoms? The crime studio's become a home to remakes and retrospectives. Look at you—shoring up your shopworn machismo with gimmick munitions and postfuturist generalities.

You're redundant. Yeah, the lot of you, and I'm here to tell you. Right now, June 17—redundant.

"What you do, that's not art. Firing officiously from on high 'cause you don't know the meaning of honorable exchange. Assuaging your guilt through your pacific generosity with a single boast—that you can die with the best of them. What does that mean here? What can anything mean in a world where life and death is decided by the gambler's throw of your pisspoor shooting abilities? I'm not here to help you pretend you're any different than the brotherhood. I'm the skeleton you strain to conceal in your own body. Your make believe ethics don't cut any ice with me, I assure you. Infantile anti-state platitudes— 'Pageantry is the stage for the unexpected shot'—so what? You can take your trite tribal arithmetic and ram it up your ass. I'm head clown among those condemned for what they've inherited—this fool's paradise of drab transgressions, cookie-cutter villains, ballistic incontinence and headshot trivia. The causes are so deep they're drowned and undone. If a single one of you beef-armed midwives of meaningless demise grew your own mind you'd end everything in a barn, but you're stopped by the self-importance of your petty mob dynastics. You and the whole crime-lite generation can go take a running jump at the shitpool of your mediocrity."

The Kid was suddenly wearing a red carnation of his own meat. He looked down at this with slow understanding, and a constellation of bulletholes began jabbing him open. He took a step backward, launching Peckinpah streamers of blood at a chart stand. A shot exposed the calligraphy of his brainfolds. Something like cheesed milk spat out of his head, hitting the back wall. The audience was on its feet, a medley of shots articulating its response. Gunblaze strobed parched faces and sparks clouded the air like sawdust. Empty housings clinked across the floor like tideshells. The lectern splintered in half. The Kid was slammed against the wall and fell to rest in a crimson pool the shape of Florida State. Peace broke out all over his face.

The gunfire died from the rear of the auditorium forward, as a figure strode down the central aisle trailing scraps of cordon tape. The attendant snipers fell silent as it dawned on them that the new arrival was the Carny, stripped to his antishocks, and letting rip at the dead imposter.

Dice "Killer" Agnew, the Kid's former cellmate, stepped onto the stage and continued firing at the body. As the Carny, he knew nothing of his own previous persona and was something more or less than human. He'd modified his Kafkacell Cannon so that the victim's point-of-view was transmitted even after death—when he killed, he got a mesmeric hit of the afterlife.

But as he shot and reshot the Kid's shredding corpse, he received nothing but grey static. He kicked the pulp with his black bulb-boots. This interloper, whoever he was, had already moved on, suiciding through the next level. The Carny had been used.

And he'd only come here to shoot the audience.

Blince slammed the phone. "Trouble at the gun bores meetin', Benny. Every goddamn year. I'll have you know better than I do them astro-monkeys take their one dumb idea and run with it to finely-crafted extremities. You know they're sellin' ammo clips with little paper umbrellas? The whole nine yards. And they call it crime like they own the notion. Goddammit I'd give my punchin' arm to see some real crime round here—not a peep outta anyone since the shit in the Mall, the heist on Deal and that explosion that wiped out the downtown precinct. Over twelve goddamn hours of styrofoam coffee, doughnuts, drawn blinds, shoutin' 'You're off the case' to maverick cops and other routine duties—them ain't the reasons I joined the brotherhood Benny, I got violence to supervise. Like the Loveless massacre few years back, remember? That guy knew how to throw a punch.

"And I ain't never liked this den. That much rocket-proof Plexiglas out front's a goddamn invitation's what it is. Place is all army—see the armory compound out back? Credit due to Geryon, but six-two-and-even his boys don't know how to fire them bloopers. And while I'm gapin' at these pansy uptown computer swatches, some idiot interferes with the Carny's presentation and he flies off the handle, shootin' the life outta the spectators. Still, I guess it saves us a barrel loada trouble re them snipers—I told you before, every bookin' offense carries its own antidote.

"Arrest the victim, Benny, that's the bottom line—wrap it up neat as a gift on Christmas Eve. And if the victim's doll-eyed and deceased our job's concluded and we can slumber easy. Think like a crook, Benny, and you can't go wrong—like if there's two fellas out there identical, same fingerprints and all, how could they use it to cheat and lie? Me, I'd use it to round up and kill dogs, but you might have different ideas. Remember that guy went and carved little anti-cop statements into his finger ends? Had the boys in the print lab hoppin' mad? Prints otherwise smooth, burned off if I recall. Then after a time the boys realized the messages contained a kind of veiled respect, first they'd received in years. Took another long while for 'em to notice the terrible spelling and realize it was the work of a cop—remember that, Benny? *Benny?*"

Blince looked about suddenly, aware of an absence.

Right about then Benny and Corey blasted through a cop roadblock in Terminal State and headed laughing for the Mall bunker.

Blood poured down the grand stone steps of the McKenna Square Assembly Hall—the closest Beerlight would ever get to a municipal fountain. The Carny strode out with a smoking rotary cannon and descended the red-carpeted stairway. At ground zero he looked at his watch, which displayed a digital image of a decaying surfer. One o'clock.

A joyrider whooped past and the Carny fired, impacts drumming across the side armor and through the cage—he got a hit of the screaming driver's view, starstreaks filling the windshield and the car pitching down into blackness, a thread of soul catching and unraveling the driver's flesh until white knuckle bones gripped the wheel. Only a whistling of wind through ribs—the view blinked out.

Well, such entertainments were fine and good but nobody ever made a living going to conventions. The Carny took his rifle apart and put the pieces in a polka dot silk bag, locating his van in the lot and throwing the bag in the rear. Then slamming a door which said CHILDREN'S ENTERTAINER, he started back to the West Coast.

Biting and tearing strips from car fenders like they were bacofoil, Specter had approached Olympus with the blurry optimism which can flow unstoppably from madness. Digging barehanded in stodgy corpses, his hopes had now born sweet fruit. The two shooters, clearly ignorant of the body's uses, had shown him the spot where Cubit was buried, saying he was welcome to it. What fools these humans were! Soon the slime would part and he'd hit the vein of manipulation he'd sought all his life—just a little deeper. He began gnashing black-ened gore aside with his teeth.

Neither of the shooters knew where to find Cubit, and they parted on the understanding that they would follow and spy on one another. Within minutes they were standing next to each other again, grudging and morose. "His deadlurk," said Parker.

"Went there earlier—zip. Danny's got an Eschaton steamer stashed—hadn't been touched."

Working on the principle that personal and cultural history are drawn by an eschatalogical attractor, an end-time which pulls events like a magnet, the Eschaton gun cut out the middleman by invoking the summational condition of the victim—usually a drift of ashes. Now and again, however, depending on a target's future plans and fortune, it would transform the victim into an all-knowing, all-powerful, floating luminous doughboy. This all-or-nothing quality and the weapon's flat ammo drum made it known to some as the "roulette rifle."

"You understand," Rosa added, "the instant we find Danny you're kissin' your shadow."

"I understan' it is your duty to try, Rosa Control."

They were strolling out of Amp Street when they saw a grey sedan with netted windows and soldered doors screeching up Sunday, pursued by cop cars. The sedan mounted the sidewalk and ploughed through dozens of trash cans—Parker saw that Cubit was simultaneously driving and shaving his face. Rosa jolted the Scatterat as Parker let rip and Cubit's windscreen and cage evapo-rated, the car slewing aside and plunging into a storefront.

Rosa took out a cop car, which hit a hydrant and bounced to a halt, a second roller batting into it. Dante Two had dashed down a blind alley, dropping his gun, and was stumbling through trash cans. At the end of the alley he hit a tall wire fence and began clawing his way upward. Parker aimed at Dante Two and Rosa aimed at Parker, like a puke chain.

A couple of minutes back, in Download Jones's deserted basement, something activated on a time switch behind the boarded-up door to the disused elevator. Ex-DoD hardware, it was a modified HAARP ionospheric storm cannon which fired a quantum electron charge up the empty shaft and out the roof of a tenement. It hit the sky, inverting the atmosphere's electron densities. Within minutes an intense electromagnetic flux saturated the city. People's hair stood on end and every particle of unshielded program data was obliterated. Monitors blanked out. Communication networks took a flap in the wind. Every digitally-aided gun in Beerlight fell dead as a rock.

"A live gun is death," wrote Eddie Gamete, "and a dead gun is life—you can put in as much effort as you like, nothing'll happen." A lesson Brute Parker had never learned—even he had allowed chips and datawork to worm into his armory. The Scatterat was a fire-by-wire and he threw this aside to reach for the slimline armani. "Don't try it!" screamed Rosa with difficulty—the wetware gun was unraveling, throwing itself from her arm with a squeal—data fluid smacked against the alley wall and the gunmeat lay flapping on the ground like a landed trout. But Parker's armani contained a digital trajectory adjustment as a build-in to the fire mechanism—when he squeezed, the whole gun fused and locked up. "This is real, Parker, a real gun!" Rosa shouted, aiming a pistol at Parker's head. She moved forward, tripping over hardware—including the Eschaton, there were four dead guns on the floor, one still twitching. "Sauer 226 automatic pistol, 9mm parabellum, fifteen rounds, no grid, no laser pulse, no sight adjustment, no funny stuff—move and you're history!"

"I love you," thought Parker, frowning.

"Danny get down from there!" Rosa yelled. Dante Two had abandoned the fence and begun climbing a fire escape to nowhere. It was a typical anodyne overdose.

When she dragged him out of the alley into Sunday she saw the last of the pursuit cops, bereft of computer guidance, simultaneously blowing each other's heads away.

Parker strolled out of the alley in time to see her move off in a cop roller, Cubit in the back seat eating fries. Rosa was breathing through her beautiful bruise of a mouth and looking the world's abyss in the eye. She'd tear out a man's heart and throw it back in his face. How *strong* that would feel.

He walked absently up Sunday. Cubit—something wrong about him. Parker had gunned loose ends before, and Cubit didn't fit the bill. He was missing that hunted, haunted look of the supplanted.

Then he drew up short. At the top of the street, where the cop den should have been, was a sort of shadow and some burned girders. He confirmed his position by looking at the other landmarks. He'd been here countless times trying to destroy this building. And there it was—a smudge for children to caper in.

A smile formed a hundred miles behind his face. "The patience of the unfired bullet is vast," he thought, "as is its strength."

In the Deal Street Highrise, Dante's book had cut out, wiped by the Jones event. He sat under the window, half-tranced.

Out of a corner shadow stepped a stranger. "Let me help you up," the figure said, reaching down for Dante's hand.

Dante was drawn easily to his feet. He looked about the warehouse. "Where's the Kid?" he asked, vaguely.

"Come away from the window, Mr. Cubit. It was a square-shouldered little theft, the sort of pioneering idiocy I thought had gone out of the world. But it's over—and you've a more pressing engagement." This was all said quite amicably by the tall man with the ashen hair and amused expression.

"And you are?"

"Eddie Gamete," he said. A white cylinder dropped silently from the ceiling and slid open—it was an elevator. "And you, Mr. Cubit, are at death's door."

PART 3

THE INFERNO

I . UNDER THE OVEN

Under the oven of the sky, Rosa's railroad car sat in dry wasteland and clanked as if it were on its way. It was rocking like a metronome. Windows exploded with the sonic bang of two borderline personalities overlapping. The girl in boots and the boy in bandages. An unequal relationship, thought Dante Two—I get the pleasure and pain. Whatever happened to codependence?

Rosa raked her steelplated nails into his chest and he ripped between agony and glory like a flashbulb. She had fixed him out of the overdose—he was a hundred smarts beyond and the walls were peeling like a pearl, strobing behind Rosa's tossing head. He sucked a breast and his tongue was lacerated by a nipple flechette, blood spurting. Desperate for leather, Rosa grasped at the nearest curtain and clenched it in her teeth. It tore down and light splashed over crimson-glistening and snow-white skin. His stomach wound opened, the bandage blossoming. Rosa was yelling ballistic technicalities each time she sank onto him, her face gnashy and flushed. Dante Two's jaw was aching from a bout of oral sex which had left him chemically altered and forensically unidentifiable. Rosa grabbed up two jolt guns and forced one into his hand, pointing the other at his head. "Charter Arms undercover thirty-eight special! Cop revolver! Sixteen ounces!" She was bucking as he tried to keep aim at the exquisite clench at the center of her forehead. "Five-shot cylinder! Three-inch barrel! Metabolic breach modification! *Now!*"

They let rip simultaneously.

Accelerating upward, they saw through the glass walls the floors folding away beneath them. "Sixteen floors," said Gamete. "Another phony office. Storehouse. Armory. Aquarium. VR deck—for countryside mainly. Surveillance room. Underwear chamber. Menagerie. Chimps mostly of course. Thinking of knocking through so the apes and underwear form a single experience. Zen room. Maze. Brig. War games. Here at any one time I run six famous court cases with a simulation adjustment so that the case proceeds according to reason. There's the Queensbury case now."

JUSTICE COLLINS (bored): Who really gives a toss one way or the other, Mr. Wilde.
WILDE: I suppose so.

"Workshop. Gallery. Lab—let's stop off here." The elevator slowed and Dante, nauseous with a sense of unreality, shuffled out after him. "Elevator doorway's lined with Zero Approach beams, by the way. If your heart weren't in the right place it'd now be splattered against the wall here. Well done—brave man. Look at this."

They were in a vast, silver, light-flooded arena of invention. "Everything in the tower runs off a Newman engine back there—but look at this shaft running the length of the chamber. Particle accelerator, as I wrote about in *Bomb Biology*. Constructed this with the intention of firing clichés at quantum speed and colliding them to see what sort of stuff they were made of. But of course when it came to it I had nothing to fire, since they've no basis in reality. And over here I'm channeling every single TV transmission simultaneously via the surveillance floor to form a single 3-D image." Gamete pointed to a transparent holographic drum in which floated something resembling a giant piece of shit. "Everything from the fifth floor upward's electron shielded, incidentally. Oh you probably don't know— someone's pulled a prank outside, electromagnetic saturation, wiped everything. Did a similar thing myself when I was younger—put electromagnetic sheets into floppies. Wipes the whole hard drive when inserted— better than a virus."

Dante had slumped into some kind of electric chair and was nursing his bruised brain.

"Neurofeedback rig," said Gamete. "Thought of it after the NLP riots. But look, this is scarcely appropriate—let's go to the Cipher room upstairs, and I'll lay out the entire jamboree in finely-crafted detail."

In the elevator, Dante glanced at him—like a dead man, it was difficult to judge his age. But it was Gamete, the man whose head had convincingly exploded, and whose body had taken residence underground before that became a fashion for the living.

They slowed and stepped into a book-lined sanctuary with rolltop desk, world globe, deep oxblood sofas, surly-guy busts, the whole nine yards. Gamete went and fixed a drink as Dante scanned the floor-to-ceiling shelves. Discs and hardcopy, everything. Here was *A Handbook on Hanging*, *Scarcity Play*, *The Imitation Fish*, *The Purple Cloud*, *Scientific Romances*, *Disaster Approval*, *The Year 2440*, *Zastrozzi*, *The Sedition Orchard*, *Walden*, *Parable of the Sower*, *The Confidence Man*, *Swastika Night*, *Saturn*

Returning, The Crystal Grenade, Allogenes, The Ninth Bridgewater Treatise, The Alphabetic Abattoir, After London, Now We Are Six, Hammer Into Anvil, The Situationist Wars, The Ice-Shirt, Small Grays Bore Me, In Watermelon Sugar, Etidorhpa, Forty-Two Million Hot Dry Rocks, The Collected Villon, Against the God Emperor, The First Third, The Castle of Communion, Heiland, Krakatit, Skin of Dreams, Heaven Contaminated and *The Telephone Book.* Here was Pushkin's '36-'37 journal, the Voynich manuscript, the *Hypostasis of the Archons*, the *Diametrics Lexicon*, the Vampire Jesus scrolls and an 1812 *Fantasmagoriana.*

And a bank of Gamete mindmaulers in hardcopy. He flipped down *Reality Scare* and read aloud. "Crime and legality—if one is not satisfied, the other will be indulged."

"The other will *always* be indulged," Gamete stated, standing beside him. He handed Dante a glass of grail.

"So Eddie Gamete, no less."

"Are you really surprised?"

"Yeah. To be honest? Yeah."

"There's a need to discard our old selves surely as a snake discards its skin—as a headcrime adept you should understand that. But then I can scarcely blame you. Come onto the terrace here—we can't be seen from outside, and it's pleasant."

Dante slipped *Reality Scare* into his coat—he had left the dead rombook on the warehouse floor—and followed Gamete into a glass-enclosed balcony garden. They sat in seats amid the uneventful air and lazy hum of synthesizer bees. Drinking, Dante noticed a moss-furred astrolabe, a pond of holographic goldfish and, on the inner wall near the conservatory entrance, the American flag.

"Think it's out of place?" asked Gamete, scrutinizing him over his glass with a hint of mischief. "It has everything to do with my story, and my time. Scientists used to do an experiment whereby a dog's repeated reward for performing a task was unaccountably replaced by punishment. The dog, knowing it would be penalized for doing well or doing badly, would become melancholic and inactive. This and other unforeseeable results were funded by taxing up to sixty percent of people's earnings. People became strangely melancholic and inactive. Humor and style together made a sandwich one molecule thick. It was known the populace would never berserk en masse—they didn't like each other enough. But advisers hadn't considered that the populace would berserk en masse by coincidence."

"Didn't the authorities swatch the problem?"

"But of course they understood it perfectly, and continued as they'd always done. The red of the blood, the whites of their eyes, the blue of the sea. You've heard of subliminals?"

The flag frilled like a Venetian blind, revealing a skull and crossbones.

Harpoon Specter was sitting dejected on the Dump rim when Blince approached. Khaki drool glazed the lawyer's chin and black birds fussed around him. "Lookin' good, Harpo," Blince remarked, setting down heavily at his side and opening a Nimble Maniac take-out. "Cubit ain't on the register, eh? Slippery customer." He gestured grinning and suggestively at the Dump. "Speakin' o' which—ha ha ha! I know I shouldn't say it about these dead guys." Blince wiped tears of hilarity from the pockets of his eyes. "Gloatin' I guess, know what I mean?"

Specter turned and gave him a small, glum look.

Blince surveyed the putrescent desolation and nodded his head. "I take a swatch at this place and figure hell I must be doin' *somethin'* right. Take a hot dog, Harpo. No? I hope and pray y'ain't on the cream horns o' some dilemma, Harp. Messes with your center o' gravity. You consider yourself a bigot, Harpo? Y'aint been a bigot over rough terrain, in hostile territory—the mettle o' your prejudices ain't been tested. You don't grow a face like mine sittin' home eatin' asparagus, I'll tell you that. Guess you'd argue you kept your bigotry in the shinin' trim o' lovin' attention. Sorry to be the one to tell ya it don't work that way—a tool's there to be utilized, not hung on the wall like some faggot bangle. Are these crows singin' in tune, Harpo? What is this racket?"

Specter glanced at him gloomily.

"Did I tell ya Benny's deserted? A turncoat! Benny! Greyest day for this community since the explosion at the brain storage facility. To think Benny's out on them mean streets feedin' alka seltzer into cash machines like some small time speed urchin. I used to think there was somethin' sacred but the gods guffawed from on high. You know somethin's newted every computer in the city? The boys are havin' to use Hecklers. I'm not makin' this up Harpo, I wish I was." He picked up a lilac piece of Dump meat and let it drool through his fingers. "Yeah, to be a real man's bigot you gotta know which side you're on and stick there till the crack o' doom and I guess your profession puts the mockers on, right Harpo? You're the shyster's shyster, I'll give you that."

Some of Blince's words were beginning to reach him, as though through a thick green slick. A favorite memory—Specter defending a holdup man. He had cited the quantum hypothesis that in an infinite universe everything will happen eventually, so the bank should have known the guy would rob them sooner or later. When, in a subsequent case, he was confronted with opposing counsel's defense of a holdup man, Specter witheringly stated that in an infinite argument, every position would eventually be adopted.

"Well—can't linger, Harpo. Me and the boys are headed out to the Rose's known domicile—first name on the rap sheet. No positive ID at the flashpoint—guess if Cubit ain't checked in here we got two on the loose, you beat that? See ya on the merry-go-round."

Blince raised himself wheezing, and lumbered off through clapping clouds of winged vermin.

Presently, Specter stood and began shuffling tortuously in the direction of the Deal Street Highrise.

2. GAMETE'S STORY

Gamete's story was the expected fender bender, but had such implications for Dante the younger man listened with acute attention.

"We're talking about a time when the activity of swapping one addiction for another was the only example of fair barter remaining in the western world. The new century had begun, in a thunderclap of generalizations. Wonderful opportunity for media bicthought, the milennium—a horse pill. And these rigorously imposed banalities were a perfect grey against which to caper. I knew I owed no morality to those who would extort it by force, but I was driven by the desire to push beyond the self-evident. In those days I was interested in the notion of innocence as a form of aggression against society. I had irony in the soul. Of course this was a turbine which propelled me into trouble.

"I was staying at the Crisco Correctional Institute for Wiseguys. I'd been told it was for my own good and I wasted two years searching for a way to believe this. When, by means of a ladder of bored-stiff guards bolted together I finished staying there, I cradled within me the bud of a headcrime.

"Maybe you're familiar with neuro-linguistic programming. The most commonly known principle is that our eyes will look in a particular direction depending on our mental activity. You can determine from this whether someone's remembering, calculating, imagining, in revery, or whatever. And it's possible to reproduce those states by consciously adopting the relevant eye position, posture and so on. I'd noticed something when dealing with authority figures—such as the clench guards, whom I'd banter with on the thorny issue of the law cartel. Their reasoning, where detectable, was often flawed, but when I pointed out their simple errors, they'd blank over. It was a very particular act of staring away at a certain angle in stony silence. I experimented with dozens of guards—it was only a matter of speaking a pertinent truth—and obtained consistent results. After my escape I kidnapped a string of cops—this was before the cop-army merger—and tested them in the neurofeedback chair you saw downstairs. The head-vice and visor work on the same principle as a motion-control camera, recording and repeating movement and position—thus, I was able to seat myself and model a bigot precisely. More importantly, I could program the device to model the mirror image of this, and thus place me in a state which was the diametric *opposite* of bigoted denial.

"How can I describe the explosion this induced? It was like perceiving everything in the world from the inside out as though it were colored glass. Millions of simple but extraordinary ideas flared through the canyons of my brainfolds and expressed themselves as geometric shapes which bloomed and shrank in midair. The faces of swine mouthed silently at me from the walls. It was touch and go, I can tell you.

"So I'd breached a state in which it seemed I could accomplish miracles of reason and creativity. Anyone with two barrels to their nose could have recognized its potential in the real world—but to me that was fathomlessly abstract. My character was flawed with an ambition. Since childhood I'd been suspected of imagination. My brain thirsted in my head. And now that it was nourished into florid activity, I began writing it all down. Speed of consciousness books. Treason synthetics, resemblist rants, torrentials and traumatism—within a year I'd written a dozen books on truculence alone. I completed *The Gobsmacker* while walking through a revolving door.

"Of course there was no money in books—they were outlawed unofficially enough for no black market to exist as yet. And as I mentioned, the honest living had been legislated to extinction, though many still pursued the wraith. Justice was starved to a vestigial irrelevance. Even that armature of the law which protected the criminal from its victim was busted. The powers were convinced the populace could live this way if they had to, and inhumanities accumulated like layers of volcanic ash. People's poverty, not their will, consented to this inarticulate nightmare. It was so intricately foolish I became convinced it was conscious—planned. Someone must have a watchmaker's skill in perdition. And I began piecing together the arcane and contraband knowledge I'd amassed since childhood. I decided to have fun with it.

"Already for years happiness had been clandestine, relegated to the tangential trespasses of vortexans, recidivisionaries and carrion angels—denizens with their veins twisted amid subterranean wiring. Horror among

twisted amid subterranean wiring. Horror among
thieves, you know the sort. This was merely clever then."

"Socketeers," Dante said.

"Exactly. Made illegal the same year as dimes. They took me in, really, under their artificial wing. I'd read a shrill news piece asking what were the solutions to all these various problems in the world, and used neurofeed-back to obtain the solutions. I hadn't realized the article was just noise, rhetorical. I think I actually wasted time posting the answers. I was soon shown my error amid much hilarity, as you can imagine. Finally, I fed those answers into a codified novel. Instead of binary it was encrypted in psychohistorical repetition patterns. This screened out those who'd detected so little pattern in past events they couldn't predict the future. Almost everyone thought it was gibberish.

"Another brief interest of mine was killing. Murder's the taking of one man's life by another—war's the other way around. This uniformity led me to seek the real dif-ferences between the two activities. I found only one— the flow of material gain. With murder it's more direct. I made it known to the authorities that they could cut out the middle man by doing it themselves. But once again I wasn't thinking practically, and hadn't taken into account that servicemen don't take a cut of the spoils. I had to admit I didn't know how a government could run a war without loss of life and still make a profit. I really didn't have all the answers.

"Oh, I was doing all this only out of laziness, and out of honor to the laziness in me. The notion of effective-ness—I could no longer extend the courtesy of respect to that illusion.

"Postmodernism was the line of retreat for the ineffec-tual in those days, but once again the law was there first.

thieves, you know the sort. This was merely clever then."

"Socketeers," Dante said.

"Exactly. Made illegal the same year as dimes. They took me in, really, under their artificial wing. I'd read a shrill news piece asking what were the solutions to all these various problems in the world, and used neurofeedback to obtain the solutions. I hadn't realized the article was just noise, rhetorical. I think I actually wasted time posting the answers. I was soon shown my error amid much hilarity, as you can imagine. Finally, I fed those answers into a codified novel. Instead of binary it was encrypted in psychohistorical repetition patterns. This screened out those who'd detected so little pattern in past events they couldn't predict the future. Almost everyone thought it was gibberish.

"Another brief interest of mine was killing. Murder's the taking of one man's life by another—war's the other way around. This uniformity led me to seek the real differences between the two activities. I found only one—the flow of material gain. With murder it's more direct. I made it known to the authorities that they could cut out the middle man by doing it themselves. But once again I wasn't thinking practically, and hadn't taken into account that servicemen don't take a cut of the spoils. I had to admit I didn't know how a government could run a war without loss of life and still make a profit. I really didn't have all the answers.

"Oh, I was doing all this only out of laziness, and out of honor to the laziness in me. The notion of effectiveness—I could no longer extend the courtesy of respect to that illusion.

"Postmodernism was the line of retreat for the ineffectual in those days, but once again the law was there first. Law always shunned the factual pursuit. Its mechanics resemble those of a dream, which has freed the dreamer from the necessities of common logic and enabled him to compress all phases of hype, hearsay and happenstance into a circular design of which every part is beginning, middle and end. Its enforcement had recently been reasserted in a volley of vagueries no one had taken the initiative to ignore. You'll find the average legislator is driven by the desire to cool his molten ignorance into some lasting obstacle, a monument if you like. The crime crisis made the powers nervous because it wasn't one they'd manufactured. I can't say I didn't sometimes want to scorch their authority in a blaze of indifference, but in truth I ducked out of the game because I was weary of reasoning with people who couldn't think without screaming. I was grey at twenty-one.

"For three years I was out of commission except for the kind of penny-ante pranks we're all familiar with. Digitally altered the major soaps and tapped into a carrier wave, broadcasting shows in which everyone cut out the bullshit—the story strands concluded within minutes of course. Chaos at the networks.

"But for the most part I was growing tomatoes, to be honest. Until the books, these deep contrivances I'd frankly forgotten about, began to kick in. Textropists, the black market, information salvage—I'd been a commodity there for a little while. But certain criminals had been making confessions in which my name figured prominently as a creative influence and the press went to work with pin-sharp inaccuracy, their conclusions meticulously unsound. I was hauled in by the brotherhood. Torture made my throat close on the truth. It seemed small enough revenge to withhold it. However, the whole thing distracted me. Should have disappeared again at once, but I had to be clever. Years wasted. More books, the fact network, that prank with the dateline—lateral stunts for which I was lionized while feeling increasingly that life was a mere exercise in exhaustion.

"It was the glamour—which thankfully wears off quicker these days. A part of me knew it was time I returned to myself and left my farewell. *The Impossible Plot* was a rock soup containing everything I'd written in a rom stack which hubbed at a satire interactive—a sub-entry maze you could wander for years. Hit the end and you're rebounded to the middle. And throughout it were clues to what I was planning—death scene and this irony tower of mine, the Villanelle. The book was a sort of schematic lament, but it somehow got a reputation as the philosopher's stone of transgression. Only one copy existed—in a safe bang in the middle of town. A gauntlet, I guess, for the young. Know my name. Earn it. I've my own monitor in the bank and saw that parodic little heist of yours. Carrying a thesaurus into a raid."

Dante was staring at the terrace flagstones, numb. And he'd promised the Kid they'd get some answers. "So I pass some facile test and get an audience."

"Don't understand me too slowly. Very few people know about this sanctuary—the plans were publicly available only briefly, through an innocent mistake. The architect thought I was a government agent. I rather quickly replaced them with the plans of an office building. The outer elevator only rises to the fourth floor—anyone trying to go higher has no business doing so. Accounts are processed for each of the concerns which are supposedly based here. There are countless safeguards—the beauty of the tower is that its battlements are internal."

"Why didn't you get out of Beerlight altogether?"

"Because there is no more infernal amusement than the spectating of civilization's bind. With the necessary defenses and discipline it is possible to observe and draw conclusions here. You know there are whole states in which original thought is no longer possible—cerebral deserts, the Fadlands. When I was a young man that absence had already swallowed the states of Panic and Ohio. Terminal's going the same way—and can't you feel it around the burned, ragged edges of Our Fair State? A virulent blandness is sterilizing even the underworld. Nothing has any flavor. You're like one of the old stylists, Cubit, which makes it all the more tragic.

"And the other reason is that, to be honest, I've become obsessed with apes. Those chimps downstairs are absolutely unbeatable, believe me. When I do finally quit this place I'll give them their freedom and laugh fondly through my tears."

"Alright, how'd you fake the hit? There's no denying you're notorious for being dead."

"Same way you did. Time breach. And hired Parker for the day."

"Folded time and sacrificed your other half?"

"Well there's the worm in the gun, Cubit—you shouldn't mistake knowledge for information. You know after the fold there's a natural and a timetripper—one's stable and one isn't. It's the tripper who's unstable, Cubit—you. You're the one should have burned in the cop's firestorm. Now don't get upset—sit down."

Dante had stood and adopted the second-stage scorpion *vrischikasan* posture in defensive surprise. He relaxed gradually, sat down as though medicated, and looked for his grail glass—he had pitched it against the wall. "Why are you saying this."

"When you looked in the book—what did you see?"

"Me escaping from a bodyvan and running round like a moron."

"And I'll bet part of the story was that this was some

other Cubit, not yourself? Why did you experience his exploits and not one of your own? Because you're no longer valid in the world."

"And you are?"

"Good point—but I won't be destabilizing into a flurry of molecules in a few hours' time. You worked on contaminated data, Cubit—messing with time's too dangerous for people to know how easy it is. A scientist once created a device which could undo time manipulations, but he was killed—probably by those who thought they'd be less well off if the natural order was restored. Also invented a car apparently fueled by depression—guy by the name of Professor Guppy."

"What happened to the device?" Dante demanded. "The time straightener?"

"Boosted a few weeks before the hit—by Billy Panacea, burglar extraordinaire, despite there being a dozen guard dogs on the premises. Nobody knows where he stashed it. The plans burned. It's absurd, but really Panacea's the only man who could untangle the mess. An opportunist fool. He's in the Mall of course, which nobody's been able to hack. Listen Cubit, it's a boneshattering shame but there it is. We've both been driven to perform somehow a crime which is unclassifiable. We've paid a price. Life's like that. Dust and a plan."

"*Damn* you and your dust!" shouted Dante, bolting up. "I don't believe a word of it! Fall apart? Fizz into a swirl of atoms? It'd be the ultimate indignity, like dying in a dodgem car! Go to hell!" He turned and stormed off.

"Cubit you bastard!" shouted Gamete, standing appalled and astonished. "What you're feeling's the last flush of attachment to the world, the last hope of effectiveness in it! You've got hours! You're ripping at the seams!"

"Tell me about your first crime."

"I was too young to remember." Rosa sat up and pushed the tangle of rubber tubing from the bed. Propping a sawed-off metabolic rifle out of harm's way, she started pulling on her shockware. "We're getting outta the loop, Danny."

Dante Two watched her operate the beautiful machine of her musculoskeletal system. She kicked aside a rubber-sheathed caulking hammer. She held his breath with a love which abandoned the human context.

"You get healing while I spray the cop car and knock off the roof sparker—we don't wanna draw fire." She leaned over and left him a kiss like a Miles silence.

Alone in the railcar, Dante Two watched the ceiling. He was having a mild infinity crisis, toxic beauty zinging like neon under the skin. Prolonged arterial love had left contusions in his flesh and garnets in his heart. Two psychoses twenty-five years in the making and this was what they made together—a pharmaceutical romance so deep it needed an airtank.

The popcorning of his brain segued into the spackle of gunhits and splash of powdering glass. Something outside.

There was a gunfight going on out there—he sat up, handcuffs snapping tight, and fell back again. At least a dozen rapid-firing Hecklers. He'd seen Rosa hook up her Sauer and Dartwall and these were letting rip. She was giving away bullets like they were coming into fashion. She was berserking. Dante Two nearly came just listening to it. Then someone winged a gasket which flew to pieces like a nail bomb, exploding a window and shredding a curtain in a turmoil of sparks. Something was on fire in here.

He'd no idea where the keys were. The cuffs were attached to a bar of the bed's headframe. He twisted over and pulled up the mattress—have to use one of Rosa's torture instruments to unscrew the nuts. There was a thing like a torque wrench she'd been using on his head—he awkwardly wrestled this from the sheets and applied it to the lugs. Screams from outside. Their tone of surprise could mean only one thing—the brotherhood. Amid the multiphonic fusillade something like a fluorescence bomb went off, denting the sidewall and rocking the railcar. The carpet was on fire, the wetware nutrient tank thundering like a boiler.

The bedhead clattered loose. He hauled it up and staggered through the smoke, lunging at what he alone considered a window. Flames climbed the stock of the metabolic rifle and the air exploded with enhancer drugs. Dante Two went towards the light.

"Submission to causes is what befell the gods," thought Parker. But was love a cause? His heart was swelling like a cancer.

Rosa Control, of the blank badge and leather hair. She was a sweet breeze drifting through the tumbleweed streets and flapping saloon doors of his mind. Her enamel skin, primitive hardware and fiery talent for the fostering of grief put him a breath away from mercy. She was exceptionally dangerous.

He was staring absently into the window of the Drilliac store which stood on the site of his old gun emporium. What a killer dies with me, he thought. He was the true spice among those whose business was the hastening of people's latter end. Should he turn up at her doorstep, percussion cap in hand? Maybe a poem about flowers and bugs? He could barely write—what were the tenses? I will knife, I am knifing, I have knifed. It was use-less—she'd punch him in the throat.

But a life lived with fear is a life lived with clarity. Any-one with the courage of his convictions for manslaughter would act. Is it a crime to want to connect with someone without a speeding bullet as the go-between? he raged. This was Beerlight, and at a deep level he knew the answer.

But wasn't he wanted anyway?

Dante climbed out of the caved-in elevator and over a stripped tank, emerging into Deal like a longcoat gun-slinger. It was a cold crime scene, old news, steamers newted by the HAARP jag. Various droll tanks and blooper emplacements sat in the streetway, targeting straightfaced at empty air.

A cop sitting on the hood of a tank bit into a hot dog and looked up in time to see the man who shot him—a death-pale guy in layers of black like the curled pages of a burned book.

Dante ditched the pistol, climbed in and started up, spinning the tank and heading downtown with the dead cop laying on the hood.

Four miles from the Mall bunker, Benny and Corey started arguing. As a side effect of strobe-hypnosis in the Mall, Benny's perceptions were flaring to beat the band. "Value's based on rarity, demand and ease of replacement," he asserted, driving. "So depending on your relationship to a person, that person can be worth everythin' or nuthin'."

"Oh, silly," Corey laughed. "That'd mean people would do *horrible* things."

She found herself sitting on the roadside, the car pulling off in an eruption of dust.

The naked figure of Dante Two staggered over the wasteland outside of town, dragging the bedhead behind him. Talk about conspicuous. While he was attached to this it would be obvious to everyone he was not only alive but in a loving relationship. He may as well have had a rifle target pinned to his back.

He had to get as far from Beerlight and the cops as possible. Rosa would be doing the same and she hated clingy men. Alaska, home of the moose and the Department of Defense's test zone.

Spanned from the jagged horizon to the city's confusion ran a rail track. Dante knew there was an armored artillery train due, bound for the brotherhood's compound. The timetable was horribly familiar from a past headcrime involving this same train. He had tied a number of chefs to the rails in the hope that the driver would speed up and hit the real obstacle placed further along, jumping the track. In the event the driver mistook the chefs' ridiculous hats and overalls for those of white supremacists and slammed on the brakes. Dante Two had had to run for his life.

Laying on the ground with the headframe on the track and the cuff chain draped over a rail, he waited. All in all the heist had not been a success. He only hoped the other guy had got a swatch of the book—anything would be more enlightening than his own so-called adventures. Was that a train coming?

4. PLACE IS KINDA QUIET

"Place is kinda quiet cuz the boys are baggin' and taggin' at the Hall. Lotta snipers died of excitement. Surprised you weren't there yourself, Rose—busy with somethin'?"

Rosa regarded the fat fucker who sat opposite. Any more meat on his face and his head would bang to the floor. A stack of burgers threw an Olympian shadow over the table as Blince systematically emptied Rosa's ammo into a tin bucket. An armed slabhead stood behind him at the locked cell door.

He voided the Sauer. "I got a sneaky admiration for you, Rose. Keep yourself to yourself or somethin' and I like that. But you mollified eighteen o' my men with these here firearms—what were you thinkin'? Not only is that murder but it makes you a goddamn accessory. Bren Dartwall .33. Whattya need with these little armor-piercin' fishies, Rose?" Blince emptied the finned flechettes from the hand cannon and dumped them into the bucket. "I presume you could see what you were doin' when you liberated 'em? So you're a material witness into the unbelievable bargain. Speakin' o' which we found a lotta stuff at your place, stolen at rockbottom prices. And a lotta blood. You wouldn't be dockin' a fugitive, would you?"

He stared at her, pouch-eyed. She stared back in the grey, faded, well-worn shock of meeting an idiot.

"Well—the web thickens. How old are you, Rose—twenty-five, twenty-six? Time to consider puttin' up your guns and dyin' into society. You got the right to a lawyer—guess you heard the bang as we drove out here, one of our rollers ran into Harpoon Specter on Radio Street, they're showin' him a bandage right about now. He'll be by later, but I'm sure we don't need to get overtechnical re the legal position."

There was no response.

"A word to the wise, Rose—this prince among men you're protectin', this fine one—he's cost a lotta lives. My boys, all them innocents at the bank, who knows who else. Your friends ain't here to help you—Jones bought the farm when Parker newted the den, Findlay the Kid's dead at the Hall—yeah, they all shot him. In a manner that was almost a threat—before the Carny had 'em rollin' in the aisles. But the hubcap o' the matter is this, Rose. I know Danny Cubit hosted the fashionable events in Deal last night—his kinda soaraway blankopathic don't need a motive, only a pretext. And it weren't too shabby, I'll give him that. But Rose—" and he regarded the table-top of empty guns awhile for the purpose of suspense, "if you don't let rip re the facts of his present location you're gonna find yourself on the wrong end of a power tool. Seems Cubit wove in a couple o' transgressions invisible to the common herd. Time shit. And books, Rose—books. I found stuff in that deposit hatch I'll never for-get—a hand sat on top o' some volume like it was swearin' to tell the truth, the shockin' truth and nothin' but. Sent the whole sick jamboree to the Pentagon, they're wise to this time shenanigan. Our Fair State's still aligned to the powers, little missy, and I'll have you know as well as I do they can screw up better than anyone. But that's so much flyin' glass—I need you to tell me what you were doin' durin' Cubit's installation number."

"Shavin' my jacket."

"Well now we're gettin' someplace," roared Blince, then stopped, frowning. "Is this what you consider rational behavior, Rose? In a jam like this one here today? I hate to be a stickleback for details—"

The door opened behind Blince and the guard stood aside—Blince turned in his chair and peered down in surprise. "Well looky here—it's a spinny chair."

In came a guy who looked like a fist in a hat.

"Get a loada the chair, Terry—it swivels."

"Fine, Henry."

"This here's Terry Geryon, Rose."

"How do you do, miss."

"Take your hat off, Terry. Terry's the armorer round here and does a little interrogation if he has the time. Trained at Benning, though he don't make a song about it. Tattooed on the other side of his skin—eh, Tell? Keep yourself to yourself, I right?"

"That's right, Henry," said the armorer, bored. "Now listen Henry there's a situation out back, we need you in the compound."

"You boys in trouble findin' the target again?" Blince coughed with laughter. "What's the tattoo of?"

"Tiamat, the primal dragon."

Blince exploded with hilarity. "He's full o' that shit. Okay Tell, I'll bail y'out. You'll have t'excuse us, Rose—me and Tell'll maybe play good cop/bad cop with you later on." He stood and picked up the ammo bucket. "But we ain't guaranteed to remember who's which."

Broken up with laughter, he left with Geryon—the slabhead guard followed, slamming the heavy door.

"Tried these?" asked Blince, brandishing a burger at Geryon as they strode to the compound. "Bilderburgers. Grey colored—they make 'em in secret—what you don't know, you know? Takin' over the market."

"That's fine, Henry. Listen, Garnishee ain't checked in—the boys checked his deadlurk and you would not believe what they found there. Books—a whole mess of 'em. Guy's a sicko."

"I always knew it, Tell."

"They never could stand takin' orders off Choke Chain."

"Put out an all-points on the bastard—shoot to kill. And gemme a soda. And baguettes. And take this god-damn bucket. So was this all you wanted to tell me?"

"No, Henry—it's the artillery train. Came in with some extra freight." They arrived at the observation deck. "See for yourself."

Blince looked down at the compound where the armored train stood hissing. The grilled plough at its prow had accreted something like a bug on a windshield. It was a metal bedhead, upon which a naked, broken man was dazedly crucified.

Benny approached the Mall bunker wearing a beard he'd shaved from a struggling hiker and a Nazi accent he'd heard on a Texan. He presented the sentry with a document bearing enough specifics to last a lifetime. It seemed natural to Benny this document had run out of the copnet at a touch of the keyboard. He'd just hit //rw.panacea.escap.mall.

The slabhead couldn't have thought slower if he'd been decaying. Finally he looked up. "Dis looks to be okay, Mistah Kurtz."

"Doctor Kurtz—please."

They were like autumn leaves around a park bench. Parker passed three burning cop cars and walked through the vivid dead surrounding Rosa's railcar. Nearby stood the roller she'd boosted, torn open on one side. The railcar itself was a wreck, warped by multiple impacts. Hecklers, Mag 10s. Panic shots.

He entered the carriage. Shredded leather curtains wafted and draped like seaweed. Light flared little details of damage. A floor of glass, a bed of blood. One wall scorched black. Her soul filled the air like solvent.

Behind a melted jawchair he found a chainsaw—and a gun case which he opened tenderly. An antique .38 special. At the front of the twentieth century, Southern anti-drug campaigners had stated that drugs were making the black population bulletproof and the cops upped their caliber. The result was the issue of this gun as standard. He chuckled fondly.

And what was this? A slimline Ingram M20 with a topped magazine—a 1000 rpm room broom, still in its thigh holster. Parker stroked the holster slowly, the demolition ball of his brain going to work. He put the gun muzzle to his nose and inhaled. Fired recently. Parker got an ecstatic rush—closely followed by self-disgust. She'd be revolted to see him here doing this.

He shut the guns away and returned the box to its place. On the bed he placed a 20mm Heavy Duty drillbit, tied with a ribbon. Greater gift has no guy, he thought, than the death of his rivals. Dante and Dante. Then he'd take her to the Creosote Palace for antifreeze in tall glasses and a skin-from-bone strip show. They had rubber chandeliers and that classy stuff—she'd see what kind of a man he was. He'd make an impression no one could hammer out.

Leaving the railcar and walking through the war zone, Parker drew up short at the sight of a hog tank standing on a dirt knoll in front of him. A dead cop lay on the hood, an ace of hearts in the middle of his face. The hatch flung open, bouncing. Dante Cubit emerged, and stared at him without a flicker of expression.

Parker made a noise at the back of his throat like the click of a trigger.

Eddie Gamete stood at the window and watched the city at work. Near Betty's Fort there was tracer fire and rippling firepools of red gold. A bigot lattice obstructed the thoroughfare. Dozens of cop rollers were drawing fire outside the McKenna Square Assembly Hall. The fuselage of a downed plane was being stripped to the girders by antlike speed urchins. The imploding road off Scanner roiled darker than dark. A bomb zombie event—some kind of small carnival—ended in a detonation which sent a firestorm flashover through the Portis Thruway into the Triangle. Gamete hoped it wouldn't be too hard for the boy—he'd seemed almost lively at the end, a real firebrand.

It had made Gamete feel old, talking to Cubit and remembering. He'd been here so long the plastic flowers were wilting. Quarried his cynicism for something edible and starved like a pup in a vault. The joke was on him—his viewpoint coincided with the facts.

Did the city have anything new to show him? Time to go?

Billy Panacea was driving his luminous cartoon car down a Mall reproduction of Prod Street when the world blew up in his face and he was lying on a metal slab in a bare white room. Benny the Trooper was slapping him round the chops and telling him to walk. The boredom was starting to fade. Sirens were blaring to beat the band. Billy had a headache which could write its own biography. And it grew fleetingly worse when he realized this moron had gotten his message.

5 . THE CROWDPLEASER

The crowdpleaser wheeled through diced rubble and skulls dry as pistachio shells, sniper fire winging off scarred armor. Inside, Dante was perusing an account of civilization's end in *Reality Scare*:

Denial. Vacuum competes with vacuum. Laws outlaw the harmless to make the effective inconceivable. Scholarly incomprehension. No questions asked. Banality given the terms and prestige of science. Ignorance worn like a heraldic crest. Mediocrity loudly rewarded. Misery by installments. Hypocrisy too extreme to process. Maintenance of a feeble public imagination. Lavish access to useless data. Fashion as misdirection. Social meltdown in a cascade pattern, consumed by a drought of significance.

Dante threw the book down, his hands tingling. He was feeling as sick as a lab rat and found that the type of several pages had transferred onto his palms. Reexamining the book, he discovered that the pages he had read moments ago were now missing entirely. Cobalt-blue pain began shooting up his arms.

He's the one alright, thought Parker, casting him a glance from the driver's seat. Look at him staring at his own arms like they're a mystery. That's not the Danny we all know.

The Dante they all knew would inflate the head of a captive mime and burst it with a stick. And this guy here had put on a pair of surf shorts—not the garments of a man who wished to stay alive.

So how to ventilate him safely and completely? Parker wondered. He could perform a meticulous stabbing or grab the cop rotaries the target had acquired as part of the tank package, but loose ends required a thorough taking apart with a Scatterat or flamethrower. There was nothing in the storage bustle but copperhead shells and antishock jackets—and the jackets were beige.

Parker knew enough about gore-belly street tanks to guess he was spitting blanks. The Malacoda was a snubbed-down Paladin with tenth-generation Chobham armor, the boast projecting showily from a bump turret. This was an M109 155mm Enigmatic Crowd Cannon, a fairlike gun of the type he deplored. Some demonic wiseacres had taken the Zero Approach principle of etheric consent and introduced a randomizer into the gridpulse—when the cannon let rip at a crowd a few people would get it who didn't deserve it and vice versa. By a tortuous route, artillery technicians had created a gun which accomplished by precision engineering what other guns did by chance.

Parker had once test-fired a portable variation—the semi-enigmatic rifle leavened the payload with smokescreens and scattershot inaccuracy and was dubbed the Patbue Cannon. But this was all academic as far as he was concerned—not only was the 155mm Enigmatic on a gridpulse but it let rip by an onboard fire-control computer and must have been newted with everything else.

He'd never botched a job before. The target didn't seem suspicious—they were just headed for the den to rescue Rosa like she was some blonde in a print dress. Like hell. The urgency he felt was nothing to do with rescue. Probably she got caught for fun. Sure, to make the crime rhyme.

"I know you're busy, Rose, I'll keep the rest o' your life conveniently brief."

Blince was flushed with hilarity when he returned to the yelling-cell. The slabhead guard hauled Dante Two inside on the iron frame and propped him against a wall, slamming the door and assuming his post as Blince sat down.

"Don't look now, Rose, but I think we found the guy who broke into your place and bled on it." Blince bellowed with laughter.

Dante Two groaned like an operagoer, trying to focus.

"Speakin' o' which," said Blince, calming down, "you got a wound we ain't noticed?"

A patch of purple blood was spreading at Rosa's chest.

Rosa took up the Dartwall gun and fired a single armor-piercing flechette through Blince's shoulder, the guard's midsection, and the door's lock housing. Blince was still spinning in his chair when she fired the second flechette pointblank through Dante's handcuff chain. Dante Two fell into her arms.

Outside, they ran slam into Terry Geryon, Harpoon Specter and a handful of laughing cops. Specter reacted like a rag doll when Rosa grabbed him and backed down the corridor, pressing the cell guard's gun to his head. "Hold your fire or the lawyer gets it!"

The air exploded with ammo and cordite.

As the public face of Beerlight justice, the uptown den's lobby was polished, clean and pacifically spacious. As a practicality it was fronted by a meter-thick wall of rocket-proof Plexiglas and no door. The reception desk was unmanned and designed for use as a trench barricade.

Trailing a razor wire fence, the tank trolled up and jerked to a stop. It was twenty feet from the den front and sat there.

In a fine show of equality, Harpoon Specter bled from both entry and exit wounds and tried telling everyone about it. But he had bitten off his tongue which lay, slick and forked, on the floor. "Quiet down," snapped a medic, slapping him.

As Specter was stretchered past, Blince gave him the thumbs-up. "You're actin' real creepy, Harpo—and I like it."

"How you feelin', Henry," asked Geryon.

"Little dizzy for a while, Tell, but the doc's patched me up here. Cornered the bastards?"

"Holed up in the system room, Henry—ain't doing any harm, everything's down—we got another thing. Take a swatch." Geryon gestured to the second floor window and Blince looked down at the silent tank. "Just came in—gun'd maybe scratch the glass."

"That's a Malacoda hog tank from downtown—musta boosted it from Deal."

"Well we're safe as houses anyhow, Henry—cannon works on a pulse grid so it's outta action."

"That a body on the hood? Kinda messed up?"

"I guess."

The turret lid popped like a ringpull and a guy climbed out in shorts and a black coat. He walked over the hood and jumped down.

He stood looking at his reflection in the den front.

"Twin brother?" asked Geryon.

Dante Two sat against the wall like a scandal-drained mayor. Hecklers hammered at the door. He wondered if the rhythm of such fusillades varied among differing cultures.

"There it is, I *told* you the time lock was a dumb idea," Rosa shouted.

"What are you so upset about? It worked, apparently—there's one of me out there who got the spice."

"Bet your bitter life there's one o' you out there—with a hog tank."

Dante Two came over to the window, and immediately suffered a kind of molecular vertigo. Dante was standing down there.

The figure turned and looked directly up at him.

"What are those, boxers?"

"Surf shorts. It's worse than I thought."

Dante saw the reflection of himself in one window and himself in another—with Rosa. Everything he'd read and all that Gamete had said was true.

There was a subterranean shift. Something clenched his guts, put him through his own opinions and out the other side. Every cell of his body shivered—he was fizzing like sherbet. What was Dante Two wearing, pajama pants?

Thank God he'd got some pants off the cell guard. Dante Two took up a clerk-issue Roadblocker and started toward the door. "Hey, where you goin' after all this?" Rosa yelled, and pointed at her chest. "Hey, I tore one for you!"

Dante Two threw open the door and took off three heads with the first careful shot.

The lawyer's wounds were closing like eyes. He sat up and flexed his malice. It was gaining strength by the minute. Criminals often return to the scene of the crime to have a good laugh. Intent on checking out the upper stories of the Deal Highrise as the blubberbrained brotherhood should have done hours ago, Specter took up his corpse and walked.

Driving the torn and rattling cop car, Panacea tried accelerating the process of getting used to it all and the relentless fact that it was real. Windshield glass sifted like sand on the aluminum floor and dusty wind howled through the cab. He gulped at detail.

Benny the Trooper seemed stern and empty as he kept the 66 Combat Magnum on the level with Panacea's appreciative gaze. It had a snubbed stainless steel barrel which shone like a spoon.

The driver and passenger were linked by two chunky silver bracelets, a chain and Benny's confusion.

Panacea kept talking, carefully avoiding any mention of VR hypnosis or autosuggestion. Benny just took it upon himself to come rescue him—a nice guy. The handcuffs were a mere disguise surely, in case they were stopped and had to mouth off—taking a dangerous criminal cross-state, brother, hence the cuffs.

But the burglar couldn't help boasting about his tactics in the Mall. The demographic handgun which Blince had taken to like a long-lost mother was a virus Panacea smelted in the smithy of his resentment. It replicated itself in the form of a gun and contaminated the streets to be taken up and fired by one and all until Panacea had the entire clench and most of the day to himself. The dial was jammed on full and he'd seen enough of the desperate and dumb to know few would learn to leave the weapons alone. "Neat, huh?" He flashed a grin into the all-too-real barrel of Benny's snub. "I can straighten everything out—I'm the one. Time breach. I appropriated something, see? Your boss's bosses'd kill for it, and only I know where it's stashed. You wouldn't need to be Blince's yes man no more. A crime doesn't have its being outside the law—the law has its being inside a crime. No new ingredients required, Benny—just reconfigure your circumstances. Everyone steals something. But make it count as an expression of your unique self and evolutionary requirements. *That*'s the arting of crime by bringing to it a sense of absolute specificity."

Benny's dirt-and-glass-powdered face took a while to respond, his dry, cracked lips unsealing like a body bag.

"What are you trying to pull?"

As Blince and Geryon watched from the second floor, another figure emerged from the crowdpleaser turret. Not for the first time, Blince couldn't believe the evidence presented to him. Brute Parker was down there—the hitman, capering around. Blince and Geryon were momentarily arrested with curiosity—what was the bastard doing?

Parker was tugging at an old streetskull which was lodged between the tank's treads and rear idler wheel. He pulled it free and ran quickly forward, squatting to scrape it across the concrete like a football-sized chalk stub—it made a thin, white mark. Working fast, he backed up and began another line.

Blince and Geryon exchanged frowns and considered it a poor bargain.

Parker was writing something on the forecourt in tall, thin strokes. He labored quickly, puffing, and lacking his usual reserve. Then he threw the skull aside, looked up at them, and pointed to what he had made.

"What's that say?" asked Blince.

Geryon looked hard. It said FLAN THROWER.

"Says 'flan thrower,' Henry. Flan's a sort of dessert or pie."

"I know what it is." Blince was momentarily expressionless. "Flan thrower. What's that, some kinda hitman slang for somethin', what *is* that?"

"Hey simmer down, Henry."

"Don't tell me of all people to simmer down, that turbo-monkey blew up the downtown den. Now he's makin' sick accusations—castin' a sturgeon at me. Look at him."

They looked down at Parker as he pointed to the message, his eyes unreadable behind mirror shades.

"He's sayin' I throw pies around the place—yeah, like

a sloppy kid without any values! Goddamit he's insultin' a police officer!" Blince whipped the Uzi barker from Geryon's belt and flung open the block window's gun-slit, letting rip one-handed. Parker ran, scrambling onto the tank and diving headfirst through the hatch. "Well he did," added Blince as the clip emptied.

The tank hatch slammed closed with finality. "Good work, Henry," said Geryon.

"Thank you, Tell. Now it occurs to me there's some-thin' I oughta tell y'about this little circumstance. Gimme another clip." Geryon handed over and Blince recycled the Uzi. "About this here twin, Tell. He ain't exactly a twin—he's kinda trouble."

Behind Dante's reflection in the rocketproof glass, Dante Two appeared. The Dantes approached each other and placed their palms on the smooth surface—the glass began to hum.

6. YOU'RE ALIVE

"You're alive then," said Dante. Dante Two found he could hear him like a bell, though the glass was surely a yard thick. "I didn't shoot you hard enough."

"Don't beat yourself up about it," chided Dante Two, gesturing vaguely to the clotted bandage, "you shot me fine—it was a fluke, some life-urge crap. You okay?"

"Terrible. Where'd you boost those gruesome pants?"

"A guard. What *you* wearing, Cubit?"

"Surfers. Are these great or what? Found 'em in the tank. You know I'm a careful shopper."

"Careful not to pay for anything, right? They ain't black—don't go with the coat."

"Yeah, well at least I got me a coat, pajama boy. I see them scars on your chest and them dents in your head from a wrench—Rosa been busy, eh?"

"I got there first."

"I bet you did."

"Hey, don't get personal."

"Personal? Remember who I am, lughead? Look at your hair, you're a mess."

"So are you, behind your face. Ain't you gonna ask how Rosa is? I'll tell you she's angry."

"Great, great. I dropped by the place, saw the carnage—came here with Parker."

"Parker, you moron? We're crayoned in at the top of his gift list."

"I know all that, believe me."

"Yeah, we're headed for a *Gun Crazy* finale with this one."

"Eh? Rosa's not some spineless bimbo."

"What? You talking about the remake?"

"Yeah, the '92. I...I prefer it to the '49."

"How can you prefer it to the '49?"

"The Joseph H. Lewis?"

"I need this? *Yes*, the Joseph H. Lewis. Remember the continuous take in the getaway car? The exhausted swamp scene with no music?"

"Ah, shove it up your ass."

"We're the same person, how can *you* prefer the remake? For that matter, how can anyone? And since when?"

"Since..." Dante looked perplexed "...This morning."

Dante Two couldn't think. There was a shrill, semi-register squealing in his head, as if his atoms were in vibration. "I don't get it."

"I know, it stinks, I'm as much in the dark as you are.

Ah, let it slide—listen I met Eddie Gamete."

"You're kidding."

"You know I don't kid. He's holed up in the Highrise grinding axes."

"Gamete. How'd he do it? What he have to say?"

"Everything and nothing, Cubit. The caper—dust and a plan."

"What?" Dante Two could barely hear him for the ringing in his ears. The image of Dante was vibrating to a blur. "What's the matter with you?"

"It ain't worthwhile," Dante stated, and as Dante Two clapped his hands over his head, the glass shattered in a spiderweb which radiated from Dante's palms.

Parker was wrong about the fire-control mechanism, which was intact and switched off. The tank's armor consisted of steel sections sandwiching layers of composite lead, ceramics, and depleted uranium which had incidentally shielded the fire-control software. The cannon was live.

Throwing a switch and finding the fire deck lit up like a pre-fall cityscape, Parker wished for the first time he'd kept up with fair gun technology. There was a grid in which squares patched in and out at random like an idling jukebox display. He hit the fire release and nothing happened. A readout flashed the words PENDING OBSTACLE/PROXIMITY ADJUSTMENT. This was the straw that broke his patience. Whatever happened to direct action?

Back in the driver's seat, Parker was reunited with his antagonisms. His mercy was swollen shut.

The frosted glass was turning to slow transparent sludge, like glue paste—Dante was pushing through it like a newborn at its caul. He waded through sluggish crests of the stuff as Dante Two snatched up his Mag 10 and backed away bug-eyed. Dollops of jellied glass plopped to the foyer floor. Dante slowed like an insect which had blundered into amber. He reached into his coat with glazed hands and drew out two Ronell rotary handcannons. Steam and weirdness were roiling around him. He waited in the lobby.

Rosa entered through the near door as a squad of bigots stamped through the far one, dressed in casual riot gear and armed to the back teeth. She hit the desk for cover—Dante Two stood his ground with Dante. The troopers lined up behind denial shields and Blince aimed a bullhorn between the shoulder crenellations of the human blockade. "You're under arrest, folks, that's all you need to know for now."

Dante Two raised his forefinger toward Dante. "Back off or I touch him on the arm!" he yelled.

"Don't be a fool, Danny," hailed Blince. "There's more to life than blowin' yourself and your enemies sky-high."

"Like what?"

"Wiseguy, eh?"

"Run, Dante," hissed Dante Two aside. "Run like the wind."

"I'm...I'm mixed up, Dante."

"About what, you moron?"

"Stay clear," he said, and glanced down—he was fizzing into the floor, losing coherence, a monument to flux. Floormatter was creeping up his legs as he seeped outward, knocking carpet-waves into solid marble.

Dante Two retreated a little in alarm—the floor was bubbling toward him like slow surf. The surface of Dante's face roiled with brownian motion and his hands had become semi-metallic, fusing with the gun handles.

"Howzabout a plea bargain?" Dante Two shouted to Blince.

"Well," chuckled Blince, "look what the chicken hauled in. I guess if you were real nice, Specter might negotiate some deal whereby you help a court to pretend their proceedings are morally acceptable."

"Will it make much difference?"

"Now easy does it, Danny boy—you got problems bigger'n a whale here—your, er, brother there looks kinda gnarly, don't he? Time's runnin' real slim. I see you back there, Rose—whatta they call this, a love triangle? More like a goddamn dodecahedron."

As Rosa opened her big mouth to yell, the Malacoda tank boast poked in through the lank glass, followed by the rest of the vehicle. As it entered it was coated in transparent Jell-O so that when it was fully through and the engine cut out, it sat glistening like a newly varnished toy. The lid popped and swung, glass string stretching—Brute Parker clambered out, becoming slathered from head to foot in waxen molecular paste as he stepped down.

He stared about and spotted Rosa, stepping toward her and gesturing to himself. "See here Rosa Control—" Uzi fire cut across the hitman and trailed a series of periods along the wall behind him. He toppled like a badly nitroed tenement block.

"We havin' fun yet?" shouted Blince, recycling the Uzi. "Now drop your weapons!" The troopers dropped their weapons. "Not you sons o' bitches!" They picked them up again, muttering and becoming bored with the exercise. "Now Danny boy, your repeated retreat into logic exhausts every possibility for dialogue, and by the look o' your familiar we don't got that kinda time, so put up your steamers on three."

"I can't," said Dante.

"I can but ain't gonna," said Dante Two.

"Up yours, fatso," said Rosa.

Blince turned back to Geryon. "What she mean, 'fatso'?"

Geryon coughed and tried to fold his face like a deckchair.

"Okay, fire when you're ready, gentlemen. And take no prisoners—we can't afford to house 'em."

Dante Two flagged his arms. "Don't shoot—it's bad luck. For me, I mean." Bullets flocked to him, tearing up the architecture as he ran and joined Rosa at the barricade desk. "Okay, honey?"

"Plea bargain?" Rosa snapped, and slapped him round the face. "Why couldn't you stick to your guns like Danny?"

"Because he *has* stuck to his guns," he protested, but was drowned out by his own rifle fire. Spent shells scattered like dragon's teeth.

Pieces of the planted Dante were being blasted to smoke.

"Get in with the chestnut gun, Terry," Blince was saying as the bullets spackled around him. He lumbered aside to reveal Terry Geryon rigged out with an Ouroboros flame thrower, a gasket on his back.

"Meet the monster, Danny boy," said Geryon. "Retaliation'll be interpreted as an act of hostility."

Dante smiled with a contempt so tight it could never be undone. Both cannons were already raised and began to whizz, the rotary barrels spinning—they blurred as he let rip. Cops were swatted to the floor, blotting like bugs. Denial shields splintered like busted wings. Soon they were all playing the fool with slamming to the wall, sputtering chest blood and other hey-watch-me antics. Dante kept on, the kick rattling his teeth out.

Then the firetrail leapt natural as lightning and Dante was weeping gasoline, a shrieking human torch, two guns blazing from the heart of the inferno. *This is living*, he thought, fire roaring through his mouth.

He clunked to his knees and the guns went out. Rustling like paper, he tipped sideways and scattered firefly embers into the air.

The pain went on, outraged at the escape attempt. Then he grasped at nothing, and snuffed out.

Something had been cut away. A surge of strength found Dante Two standing from behind the armored counter and taking sure aim. What did the Kid always say? *Be* the target and you can't miss. Dante Two was shooter, gun, bullet and victim. The round smacked through the Ouroboros gasket and Terry Geryon went nova, most of his flaming limbs hitting the ceiling and sticking there to burn.

Everyone persevered to manifest the idiosyncracies of bloody mayhem but the shooting was getting old—even Rosa's mind was wandering as she fired a Heckler. What was this about again? "Ah, we're back in the loop, Danny," she realized, exasperated. "Look at us. What is this? Why are we here?" It was like quitting a habit—the city had dragged them right back in.

Dante Two's composure evaporated. He got a vision of the city as a gigantic spider, its legs reaching around the world to clutch it like an egg. More spiders in the egg, the packed superdensity of which was the source of gravity. What else was there but the spiders in their circle? Maybe the habit isn't in us, he thought. What if we're a habit that the world doesn't want to let go? Crazy thinking.

Blince aimed the bullhorn around a corner of the Malacoda hog tank. "Surrender now and I'll forget I ever said this."

Rosa and Dante Two were getting up to leave when the tank completed its proximity adjustment, swiveled the boast and let rip, filling the lobby with random, galling interference.

7. CLINGING ON

Clinging onto the cables and wall like a lizard, Harpoon Specter climbed the outer elevator of the Deal Highrise. The lawyer's hydra-headed resentment lit his way and drove his body. Who was up there, scratching in the half-light?

Above the fourth floor, the shaft was blocked solid. The elevator doors were part-way open, forced from inside. He slid silently through.

A warehouse of small spiders and big dolls. One of the big dolls was moving—a man stood by the far window. Tall and white-haired, he crouched down and picked something off the floor. A book done up in black vinyl. Specter drew a snub gun and advanced on him.

The hitman awoke in rubble. The hardened glass crust which covered him popped and exploded as he sat up. Running through his habitual wake-up inventory, he surveyed his surroundings. The tank. Cop bodies. Blince under a beam. Pieces of Geryon. Shadow of Danny. Where was Rosa?

He clambered through trash to the rear door, opening the tank-issue antishock jacket. Walking down a corridor, he assessed the damage. One round had penetrated, but this wasn't the victory. He'd never let his principles slide for anyone—he wanted to show Rosa the anti-jacket like a trophy and tell her, "See here, Rosa Control, I wore beige for you." The corridor turned sharply and he slammed straight into her.

Something was very wrong. He looked down to find her steel-plated nails were buried in his chest. She shoved the claw further and a rib snapped directly over his heart. She was staring right into his face, her fingers buried to above the first joint. She pushed.

"Rosa," he said in a hurt tone.

"Leave it," someone said behind her. Parker looked to see it was good old Danny Cubit, who was bleeding from the nose, ears and spirit. "Moron doesn't even work for himself. And getta loada the jacket."

Parker didn't dare move a muscle. He could see every pore in her face. Rosa clutched a little, looking him in the eyes. "Fuck off," she whispered, and gave him time to think about it. Then she let go—he dropped like a sack of garbage. She was already gone, with Danny.

"Going up," said the tall guy, and the glass elevator started to rise.

Specter saw armories, plunge pools, computer rooms and forests full of monkeys slide on down as the tall guy spoke.

"Swank steamer—messy at close range, I think you'll find. My name's Gamete—Eddie Gamete. And you are?"

Specter said nothing.

"Beige pants. A lawyer, am I right?"

Specter blanked him, staring off a little in stony silence.

"Don't be ashamed, there are worse professions. Those who mince cows and pee into the mix, for instance. Door-to-door merchants who won't go away and force you to throttle them and undergo the trial of disposing of a gaseous cadaver. Death himself, rapping at the window with a bony knuckle when you're at the point of orgasm. Met him once. Turned out to have a constant stupid smile on his face and a clapper in his chest—like in a bell. Of course his rib cage just clattered when it swung, didn't ring ominously as it was intended. Felt sorry for the bastard. Dry, you see? Offered to line his inner wall with iron. Mythic resonance. Death-knell. Charged him thirty large. Hammered the pig ore myself in a forge bellowed by the screams of a hundred chefs. Those same chefs which were then being thrashed and tormented by midgets would later form an idiosyncratic religion in the unshakeable belief that they had visited hell—which in a sense they had. I came away from the experience with a new definition of myself and my abilities—I never laughed so much before or since. And of course I had the chest wall for the reaper, polished to perfection. What I never explained to him, however, was why I also knitted in a thick layer of wool which muffled the bell, the net result being that he was both heavier and angrier than before. Think of the frustration. So you're better off than some, yes? Top floor. After you."

The door slid open and Gamete gestured in deference, but Specter waved him through sharply with the gun. As Gamete walked out, the lawyer saw a scene of urbane luxury beyond. A dunce shot and it was his. He raised the gun at Gamete's retreating back—stepping out of the elevator, he passed through the Zero Approach screen and flew to pieces like shit hitting a fan.

Back behind the big desk. Some boys coming back all laughs from the McKenna cleanup had helped him off with the fallen beam, and later, wandering by and seeing he was still recumbent under gravity, helped him up. The villains of the piece looked to have made off in the hog tank which was gone when he awoke and Blince never felt better than after successfully resisting the clammy advances of a 155mm rocket shell. Once again he was the eyes and ears of chaos. Reports flooding in of hundreds of chimpanzees running berserk at the Deal crime scene. Scene boys taken totally by surprise. And a package arrives by the good old SS Mail in a shielded microtruck. Brown with blood and what's inside but a bound thesaurus and a scrawled note:

Cubit's book.
T. Garnishee

Could you beat that? Blince scrolled the volume. "Reward, deserts, proof of regard, shield." This stuff cracked him up. He'd jet it off to the Pentagon like he did the first one. Wouldn't they get a bang out of it when they put them together and realized it wasn't two copies of a book, but the same book duplicated by time shit?

"Well, well, well—whattya know." Blince pulled the Choke Chain file and flipped a photo. There it was—the doglike tenacity in those features. "Always knew you had it in you, Tredwell. There's a mess o' commendations comin' at you full tilt." He propped the portrait against a coffee cup. "Look at you sittin' proud. We understand each other, don't we? Leave civilization to its own devices and it's only a matter o' time before it tosses its pacifier outta the buggy. You said a mouthful there. In an emergency they're expendable, ain't they? And ain't these past two years been a state o' national emergency? Bet your sweet life. Ah, you know me, Tred—danger rears its bright face and I'm a rip-lettin' fool. Danny and them others ain't wakin' outta this one, you know why? Some nightmares you get hooked on like trash TV—gets behind your face. Attitude don't count for zip—all we need's a name. Hell, you think I'm playin' devil's apricot here? Looka that—trigger finger's still got a dent. Guess all the book learnin's research, eh Chokey, takin' your work home? Nuthin' wrong with that, knew you hadda have your reasons. Yeah, there's a reason for everythin' but opera and guilt. I right?"

A bug stop-started across the desk—Blince slammed a palm at it, folded his hand and slapped the morsel into his mouth.

Hand on heart, Brute Parker wheeled through the Thruway and listened to the birdlike trill of tank armor ricochet—kids hung on the boast and molotov flare-pools bloomed like rosebeds. Love sure burned a layer off your expectations. "He who fights and runs away," he thought, ramming through a roadblock, "than never to have loved at all."

"A lot can happen in a day," Rosa said. She'd never been in a real, hooked-up railcar before and couldn't believe it was about to move. Hunkered down behind a conifer stand of dud and dusty Hellfire missiles, neither of them could get it through their heads that they were escaping. It was like waking from a dream of Charlie Chaplin to find yourself merely clinging to an aircraft escape door in the freezing Atlantic. Shame about the other Danny though, thought Rosa. He'd seemed kind of mature at the end—a man you could get your teeth into. "I guess we're in real trouble this time."

The armored train shoved, and started slowly to roll. Light and shadow passed over Dante Two's bloodied face. "Rosa," he said, his voice slurred by the enigmatic shrapnel lodged in his brain, "are we nearly there."

The cop car perched on the edge of nowhere.

Panacea—virtual escapee and erstwhile savior—looked at the passenger door swinging loose in the wind, sand hailing through the shot-up cab. He'd done a fine job explaining how Benny was really the crook and he himself was the force of order. Such a fine job Benny had shot him through the lung, blasted the cuff chain and run panting into the wasteland.

Panacea was collapsed against the dash—he could see his own magenta blood glitter amid the glass bits on the floor. It was exactly as he remembered it.

Another clamp of pain and he was spluttering, laughing blood. He'd been told there'd be a moment when life got better. The pain was real, even killing him—it was paradise.

And the Pentagon ignited, going up like a pirate flag.